LEAVE BEFORE HE KILLS YOU

JULIETTE DUNCAN

FOREWORD

Hello! I'm so glad you've purchased a copy of this book, and I do hope you enjoy it. If you haven't already received my free book, "Hank and Sarah - a Love Story", go to http://www.julietteduncan.com/subscribe to get the ebook for FREE, and to be notified of future releases.

GLOSSARY

NOTE: This book is set in Australia, and therefore Australian spelling, terminology, and phrasing have been used throughout.

Australia US explanation

Girl Guide - Girl Scout

Face washer - Flannel/ washcloth

Caravan - Trailer

Annexe - A separate canvas room attached to the caravan (trailer)

Dreamtime stories - The Dreamtime is a term that describes unique stories and beliefs that are owned and held by different Aboriginal groups within Australia.

Accommodation - Accommodations

Cubby house - Children's play house/tree house

Chooks - Chickens/hens

Two storey home - Two story home

PROLOGUE

Pivotal moments that change the course of your life. We all have them. I've had way too many. This is one of the biggies...

Reversing down the driveway of the cottage my husband and I had moved into only days before, I gripped the steering wheel and fought the heaviness in my heart.

I loved my husband. I didn't want to leave, but I had to.

He could return at any moment. If he did, he'd most likely kill me. Since moving into the house, I'd pretended everything was fine. But as I unpacked, I also repacked. If he'd known what I was doing, I might not be alive now to tell my story.

I had to get out of town, and quick.

The plan that had evolved over the past few days was now in motion. There was no turning back. I felt sick in the pit of my stomach.

Early that morning, my husband had left for a tennis tournament in Brewarrina, the closest town to Bourke, the tiny outback town in New South Wales where we'd lived for the past year. Brewarrina was an hour's drive away. Not far enough.

With our three daughters, aged five, two, and three months, I would drive an hour and a half in the opposite direction to the town of Cobar, ditch the car in a derelict barn, and then take the twelve-hour bus ride to Adelaide. That was leg one. If we made it there without him finding us, we'd be on our way to safety, and a new life without him.

But our old Holden station wagon was well-known in Bourke, and any number of my husband's friends could see us driving out of town. There were no alternative routes. At least not one an old car like ours could take. I prayed no one would notice.

Could I pull this off? For my three daughters, I had to. If we stayed, we were in danger. Each day, he grew more volatile and unpredictable. I feared for my life.

As I pulled away from the house, I brushed tears from my eyes. I grieved for him. He was losing not only his wife, but his three little girls. But I was doing the right thing. He'd had so many chances to fix his alcohol and drug problems, but each time he drifted back to his old ways. I'd already left four times. This time I couldn't go back.

Hot tears streamed down my cheeks. My throat tightened. For the sake of the girls, I had to pull myself together. How could we make it to the other side of the country if their mother was a blubbering mess? I had to be strong.

I dried my tears and drove through town, hands fixed so tightly to the steering wheel my knuckles were white. It was the right thing to do, although it went against every grain of my being. Marriage was for life. Ordained by God. Until death do us part. The problem was, my death could come prematurely if I stayed.

He wouldn't mean to kill me. It would happen in a drunken rage, but it could happen at any time.

I'd done everything possible to avoid this moment, but now I had no choice.

Fleeing across the country and going into hiding to protect my own life and that of my three young daughters, one of them still a babe in arms, was the only option.

CHAPTER 1

To outsiders, my childhood would have appeared normal. A father, a mother, three children, of whom I was the eldest, a dog and a cat. And I guess it was.

I grew up in the northern suburbs of Sydney in the 1960's and 70's, when bread cost less than thirty cents a loaf and mobile phones and the internet were not yet heard of. Back when it was safe for kids to play in the street without supervision and to walk to their friends' places instead of being dropped off and collected by their parents.

My mum and dad strove to provide the necessities of life for our nuclear family. We weren't rich, but we didn't go without. Our house, a modest three-bedroom home, backed onto the bush, and every morning, just as daylight peeked through the venetian blinds, kookaburras, perched in the surrounding gum trees, woke us with their laughs.

My dad was always fixing or making things. I can remember once, maybe twice, in my whole childhood, when he sat down on the couch and watched television with us. Every night after work, he'd have dinner and then retreat to the garage to work on some project or other. He was extremely handy and could do almost anything, but whatever he did, he did perfectly. Sometimes I'd watch him out of curiosity; other times I had no choice, like when he worked on my first car. He was a mechanic and I was his apprentice, whether I wanted to be or not.

He could never sit still and didn't like it when others did. He was a perfectionist who lacked patience, and he quickly exploded when things didn't go to plan. My siblings and I learned early on to keep out of his way when he ranted, raved, and swore.

I'm not sure how, but we always took regular vacations, and I have fond memories of long summers at the beach. I'd like to say they were lazy days, but no. My dad loved fishing, and it followed that we did too. He taught us to rig our fishing rods, how to cast into the ocean, lake or river, how to remove any fish we caught from the hook, and then, how to scale, clean, and fillet them. I would much rather have spent my holiday lying in the sun reading a good book.

You might wonder where my mum was in all of this. It's probably obvious from my lack of mention that she took a back seat to my dad. She was quiet, meek, and pretty much did whatever he told her to. She was a gentle soul and a good mother.

Like most mums, she ferried us kids to all our extra-curricular activities. I played netball, swam in a squad, was a Girl Guide, and for a short time, a marching girl. When older, I took ballroom dancing classes and learned the guitar. My life was never boring or dull.

At age fifteen I started working a part-time job at one of the local garages. That was back in the day when garages offered full service, so I filled tanks, washed windscreens, and checked oil, water and tyres until my hands were black and my clothes reeked of fuel.

The most pivotal event of my life also happened that year. One of my close friends invited me to her church and youth group. I accepted and went with her. Mum had sent the three of us kids to Sunday School when we were younger, but I'd never been to a church that was alive and preached the gospel in a way that was relevant and meaningful. I immediately felt God's call on my life and one night, to the tune of "Just As I Am", I responded to an altar call and invited Jesus into my life. My heart was open and needy. God filled a void I didn't even know I had, and my commitment was genuine and real.

God, the youth group, and church soon became my life.

And then I discovered boys! The youth group was full of them, and I did the rounds. I wasn't fussy—as long as they liked me and were presentable. I fell in and out of love at the drop of a hat, until the day I met Greg.

We met at a junior high camp where we were both leaders, and the moment my eyes landed on his twinkling blue ones, my heart did a backflip. I knew I had to get to know this quiet, unassuming guy.

The first night, when the dinner bell rang, I timed joining the line so I'd be right behind him. My heart raced as I searched for courage to introduce myself. I'd never had to do that before. I cleared my throat and stepped to the side and smiled. "Hello, I'm Julie. You're one of the leaders, aren't you?"

He smiled, and the dimple in his chin caught my attention. "Yes, I'm Greg. Nice to meet you." His voice was as soft as his honey coloured hair.

"Is this your first camp?" I asked, knowing full well it was.

His eyes danced. "Yes. How can you tell?"

I shrugged. "I haven't seen you at one before, so I guessed."

"Oh." His eyes held mine and my heart took off again. "I'm guessing this isn't your first."

"No, it's my third. I love coming. The kids are great, and the leaders aren't too bad either." I let out a nervous chuckle. I hadn't meant to flirt. It was a Christian camp, after all, and the rules stated that leaders weren't to fraternise with members of the opposite sex. I wasn't fraternising, I was just being friendly.

We inched forward, and when we reached the counter, he stood aside and let me go first. He wasn't only good looking, he was a gentleman. We filled our plates and then sat together and chatted. He was at Bible College studying to be a minister. I was at University studying to be a teacher. He told me he came from a country town where he'd lived with his mother and his older brother before going to college. His dad had died in a road accident when he was two, and his mother never remarried. She dealt with her grief by focusing her whole attention on raising her boys.

My heart went out to him, his mother and his brother. "That's so sad. She must love you so much."

He smiled, and his blue eyes twinkled. "Sometimes a little too much, if that's possible."

"She must miss you."

"Yes, but it was she who encouraged both me and my brother to study for the ministry."

"She must be proud."

He smiled and nodded. "I think so."

The more we chatted, the more he captivated me. He was everything I'd ever dreamed of in a guy, and I dared to hope that he might be falling for me as quickly and hard as I was falling for him.

Over the next few days of camp, either by accident or design, we bumped into each other often, and by the time it ended, I was in love. Greg had never had a girlfriend, and he was shy when we started dating. Apart from God, his main focus was his study. I didn't have a problem with that. I loved that he was studying to become a minister, and that he loved God so much he felt led to serve in that way.

The first time he held my hand, a silken cocoon of euphoria enveloped me. When our lips brushed for the first time, a deep sense of longing to be held and kissed properly by him filled me. The anticipation was almost unbearable. But Greg had been raised to do the 'right' thing—*'For this is the will of God, your sanctification: that you abstain from sexual immorality; that each one of you know how to control his own body in holiness and honor...'*

So, no passionate kissing, and my longing remained unfulfilled. I had to learn patience, something I didn't have a lot of, but Greg's commitment to purity just made me love him more.

Sometimes we went out on our own, but mostly we went out with friends. He said it was better that way. And so, our relationship progressed slowly, but I was happy because I believed that one day we'd marry. I was hopelessly in love, and I thought he was, too.

After a few months of dating, the college year ended and Greg was heading home for the Christmas break. My heart was heavy anticipating six weeks without him, but when he invited me to come to his home town to stay for a week, I couldn't hide my excitement.

I spent Christmas with my family, and two days later drove the seven hundred miles north in my one-hundred-dollar car. My dad had been less than happy for me to drive such a distance on my own in such an old vehicle, but I was adamant. I was nineteen, after all, and I could make my own decisions. In the days leading up to my departure, he gave me a crash course on what to do should the car break down. But I had faith in my old Morris Major, and it didn't fail me.

My heart was in my throat when I reached the outskirts of Warwick twelve hours after leaving Sydney. Had I done the right thing? What would Greg's mother think of me? Would things still be the same between us in his home environment? I sent up a prayer as I checked the directions he'd given me.

I found the street and pulled up outside a small house with a white picket fence. Taking a deep breath, I climbed out, but as I walked slowly to the door and knocked, my chest tightened and my hands grew clammy, and not because of the midsummer heat. When Greg opened the door and smiled, my butterflies settled. It was going to be fine. I didn't know what I'd been worried about.

His eyes glinted as he stepped forward and drew me into his arms. Contentedly, I rested my head against his chest. He'd missed me as much as I'd missed him.

For a long moment, I floated on air as I returned his hug. He finally pulled away and our gazes met and held. My heart flipped again. I loved everything about him, from his golden, wavy hair, to his sparkling blue eyes that held an element of mischief, and the dimple in his chin that appeared every time he smiled. He lowered his head and kissed me lightly on my lips. Although I longed for more, I was happy to wait. Just being with him again was enough for now.

He gazed into my eyes and smiled. "How was your trip?"

"Long." I let out a nervous laugh.

He took my hand. "Come and meet Mum."

I clung to him, enjoying the feel of his hand in mine as he led me along a short hallway to the kitchen.

His mother, a short, attractive lady with wavy hair just like his, although hers was tinged with grey, turned around and smiled. She wiped her hands on her apron and stepped toward me. "Julie, nice to meet you."

"It's nice to meet you too, Mrs. Thomson." I returned her smile and took her outstretched hands. So far, so good. My family had never been one to show much physical affection, and I wasn't sure whether I should kiss her or not. In the end, I decided against it and just squeezed her hands.

"Would you like a cup of tea? You must be tired after that drive," she asked, her voice gentle and kind.

"That would be lovely. Thank you." I smiled, relieved that all was going well so far.

She let go of my hands and proceeded to make a pot of tea. Greg motioned for me to sit at the small kitchen table. I pulled out a chair and carefully sat down. He sat opposite. My gaze wandered around the room. So neat, so tidy. I'd never stayed in a home like this before. Our kitchen at home was often noisy and messy.

She carried the teapot, complete with knitted tea cozy, to the table, and then poured the tea into three dainty porcelain cups resting on matching saucers. She joined us at the table and then offered home-baked cake and cookies.

I tried to use my best manners. My grandmother had spent many hours teaching me and my siblings how to conduct ourselves when out. Not that we were without manners, but we rarely went places where they were on show. I took my cue from Greg and used the napkin to wipe my mouth, sipped my tea daintily, and spoke quietly.

As we engaged in polite conversation, I wondered what the next week would be like. Would I survive in such a quiet house?

Greg showed me to my room. It was exactly how I expected it to be—neat and tidy, like the rest of the house. A carefully folded light-blue towel and face washer sat on the end of the single bed. I guessed it must have been the bedroom of Greg's older brother, David, who was now married and had spent Christmas with his wife's family. Boys' books, like *Treasure Island* and *Huckleberry Finn*, filled the bookshelf along with sporting trophies and pennants.

"I hope you'll be comfortable in here." As Greg stood in the doorway and held my gaze, I longed for him to hold me again, but in his mother's house, under her watchful eye, I figured the likelihood of that happening was next to none.

I smiled. "I'm sure I will be."

"I'll let you unpack. Come out when you're ready."

"Thanks." I sat on the bed and asked God to bless our relationship and to help me connect with his mother. Although she'd been polite and welcoming, I also felt she'd been assessing me, and I hoped I'd passed.

Over the following days, Greg showed me the sights of his home town and the surrounding countryside. We took long drives into the country, stopping for coffee and cake at quaint cafés in sleepy towns, and taking picnics along creek beds and shady parks. Sometimes his mother came with us, but most times, she stayed home.

One night during dinner, the phone rang. It was for me. Surprised, I took the receiver from Greg's mum and said hello. It was my friend, Leigh. We'd both decided it was time to move out of our family homes and our plan was to become flatmates. I was tired of being controlled by my father, and Leigh had similar reasons. Our mutual friend, Brian, had no choice but to move out, as his parents were shifting to the country and he was attending University in the city. We were all members of the same church and youth group, and we got on well, so it was just a matter of finding a suitable place we could afford.

They'd promised to keep looking while I was away. I was hopeful they'd found something—why else would Leigh be calling? And they had. A two-bedroom flat near the university Brian and I attended, and not far from Leigh's work. After getting the details, I agreed it sounded like a good deal and returned to the table with a smile on my face, where I shared the good news with Greg and his mum.

The week passed too quickly and before I was ready, it was time to leave. The only positive point was that Greg would be returning to Sydney two weeks after me, and I had a flat to move into.

On the morning I left, he walked me to the driver's side of my car and slipped his hands around my waist. We were partly hidden from his mother who stood on the small porch at the front of the house. His eyes brimmed with tenderness and passion, and I desperately wanted him to kiss me. He lowered his face and brushed his lips against mine. "I'm going to miss you, Julie." His voice was like honey and his lips as sweet as wine. I thought my heart would burst.

I smiled into his eyes. "I'm going to miss you too. Thanks for a wonderful week."

My heart pounded as he pressed his lips against my forehead and then pulled me close and hugged me. "Drive carefully."

"I will." I pulled back and held his gaze for a moment, then forced a smile and slid onto the driver's seat, biting my lip to stop my tears from flowing. I started the engine, smiled again, and drove off. The tears that had threatened to fall now slid down my cheeks and blurred my vision.

For the next twelve hours, my mood fluctuated between euphoria and heartache. I longed to be with Greg constantly, but I knew that was such a long way off. I needed to be patient and not push. As I played worship songs on my cassette player the whole way home, I asked God to give me an extra portion of patience and to help me grow in my spiritual walk with Him so that I would be fully equipped to support Greg as he entered the ministry.

The day after I arrived home, I started packing. Within a week, Brian, Leigh, and I moved into the flat. For the first time in my life, I felt free.

Greg returned a week later and we picked up where we'd

left off, but he warned me that the year ahead would be challenging. As well as his study, he was being assigned to a church as a student minister. He said we probably couldn't see each other as often as we had been. I said I understood and prayed once again for patience.

The year began, and we both dug into our study. As he'd already warned, our time together was limited to one or two evenings each week and a few hours on weekends. I'd increased my hours at my part-time job to pay my rent, and he had his church commitments. The days we were apart went so slowly. I struggled to focus on my study and not think of him continually. I treasured each moment we had together.

Toward the middle of the year, I began sensing something was bothering Greg. He didn't want to go out and he didn't call as often. I thought he was worried about his exams, but how wrong I was! Yes, he was focused on his exams, but that wasn't the problem. After a year of dating, he ended our relationship. His excuse was that he needed to focus on his study. I knew that wasn't the only reason, but he refused to give another.

My misery was so acute it became a physical pain. All my hopes and dreams, dashed. Gone, just like that. I couldn't believe this had happened. I thought we were going to get married.

I harassed him because I needed to understand. We'd been rock solid. Why did he break it off? One day, he agreed to meet, and he gave in and told me. *His mother didn't like me. She didn't believe I was the right girl for him.* I was dumbfounded.

"What...what do you mean?" I'd never had anyone say they didn't like me before. It was like being punched in the stomach. I felt winded. Ill.

His eyes moistened and he rubbed my arm. "I'm sorry, Julie. You wanted to know, so I told you the truth."

I dabbed my eyes. "How long has she not liked me?" I could barely speak.

"Since that phone call."

I frowned. "What phone call?"

"The one about the flat."

My frown deepened. "I don't understand."

"Mum's a very conservative woman. She was disturbed to learn that you'd move away from your family when you didn't need to. And she was even more horrified that you were moving in with a boy." He grimaced. "It didn't matter that he was just a friend."

I blinked, and then my blood boiled. "Why didn't you stand up for me? You said you loved me."

Tears welled in his eyes. "I tried, but she hounded me. Every night for months. In the end, I had to choose. It was you or her. After everything she went through for me after Dad died, I couldn't do it to her. I'm so sorry."

It was too much. I was gutted. I shook my head, turned and fled. I don't know how I managed to drive home. When I got there, I threw myself on my bed and wept.

It was over. Nothing I could do or say would change his mind—he'd made his decision and was going to stick to it.

My world had fallen apart. I grew depressed. I barely ate. I struggled to get out of bed, and I almost failed my exams. Only my best friend, Sandy, understood how I felt, but she couldn't change what had happened.

I pleaded with God to make Greg change his mind.

I asked Greg if we could meet again, but he said it was

better we didn't. It would only make the breakup harder.

Days and weeks passed, but I couldn't pull myself out of the deep depression I'd fallen into. I had to do something. I couldn't live near Greg and not be with him.

My family had moved interstate a few months before Greg and I broke up and were now living in Brisbane. I decided to join them. And so, after Uni finished, I moved the eight-hundred miles north to Brisbane, Queensland, and returned to living with my family.

Another pivotal moment in my life.

Brisbane didn't impress me, however, in the frame of mind I was in, nowhere would have. Compared to Sydney, it was hot and humid, and I knew no one other than my family. But the only way I'd ever get over Greg was to not be near him, so I made an effort to get on with life. I found a church and made some friends. I got a part-time job and joined a netball team. I tried to get over Greg by filling my days so I had no time left to think about him, but in the still of night, images of him played through my mind, tormenting me. I didn't know how to stop them even though I prayed continually for God to help me.

The new year finally began and I started at a new university. Coming in half-way through the course was a struggle. Both the Uni and the course were different from what I'd been used to and I almost pulled out. The only thing stopping me was that I didn't know what else I'd do, so I figured I may as well stay.

Essentially, nothing had changed apart from my location. I started dating again, but not because I wanted to. The only person I wanted to date was Greg. Dating others, I thought, might help me get over him.

CHAPTER 2

wo years after arriving in Brisbane, I graduated as a primary school teacher and received my first posting in a town seven hours north of Brisbane. I knew nothing about the town and knew no one in it. But it was a new beginning. Another chance to leave Greg behind and have a fresh start.

I had to—Greg had started dating someone else. Someone more suitable. It was over between us, although I doubted I'd ever find anyone I loved as much. It had been more than two years since we'd broken up, but he still dominated my thoughts. It was wrong. I knew it, but I just couldn't leave him behind. I couldn't understand why God had allowed this to happen. I'd been positive Greg was the one for me, and although I never said it aloud, my trust in God to find my life partner began to wane.

It was mid-January when I packed my car and headed north. I'd thought Brisbane was hot and humid—it had nothing on Gladstone. Just south of the tropics, humidity hung in the air like a wet sheet. I'd never felt anything like it before. When I reached the motel I'd pre-booked, I didn't want to go outside, but I had to. There was a lot to do before school began. For starters, I had to find somewhere to live.

Two days later, I moved into a flat with another new teacher. Janine came from a nearby town and she knew the area well. It was strange sharing with someone I didn't know, but we got on well enough, although I soon learned she didn't share my Christian values. She encouraged me to go with her to Friday afternoon drinks. I had no interest, it wasn't my scene, but to keep her happy, I went once and drank lemon, lime and bitters, my go-to drink at the time.

I was assigned a Grade Three class and thought I'd have no trouble handling seven and eight-year-olds. But Gladstone was an industrial town full of itinerant workers and their families, and most of the children went to school only because they were forced to. They had no interest in learning. Like most of the other teachers, I spent the majority of my time disciplining naughty children, and the well-planned lessons Janine and I stayed up all hours preparing went by the wayside.

As Janine went home most weekends, I often took long walks on the nearby beach to help pass the time. I'd started attending one of the local churches, but although I'd made a few friends, I was still very much on my own. I missed my friends from Sydney. They were so far away. Had I made the right decision? Would I have gotten over Greg with their support if I'd stayed? Now, here I was, far away, and lonelier than ever.

I spent hours sitting on the beach reading my Bible, praying and journaling. I was desperate for God to give me direction for my life. I didn't enjoy my job, even though I'd spent four years studying and training for it. My heart just wasn't in it. But as I dug deeper into the Word, I felt God calling me to start a Christian group for the kids at school. At last, I had something I felt passionate about. After meeting with the principal and gaining his approval, I connected with the Inter-School Christian Fellowship Organisation and started planning. I prepared fliers and handed them out. I planned fun activities, practised playing songs we'd sung at the Junior-High camps, and prayed for God to bless this new project.

When twenty kids turned up that first afternoon, I could barely contain my elation. I'm not sure whether they came because they wanted to hear about Jesus, or because I'd offered free food. I didn't care. They came, and that's all that mattered. I gave my heart and soul to those kids, and when one by one, they gave their hearts to Jesus, I knew that God had finally given me a purpose. I much preferred talking about God and His love than trying to teach multiplication and grammar to kids who couldn't care less. I'd found my niche—nurturing these kids in the ways of the Lord gave me great joy and purpose.

I began enjoying church again and started spending time with some of the other young adults. One night, at the end of an evening service, Lisa, one of my new friends, rushed over and dragged me toward this guy I guessed was her brother. She'd told me during the week he was coming to visit. I'd gotten the feeling she was trying to match-make. I wasn't sure how I felt about that, but my interest was piqued.

When he turned around and our gazes met, I was more

than interested. Dark wavy hair, smooth olive skin, and the most alluring eyes I'd ever seen. My pulse skittered.

Lisa pushed me toward him. "Julie, this is Joe. Joe, this is Julie. She's a teacher."

My cheeks warmed as I stopped in front of him.

His eyes widened and a smile flitted across his lips. "A teacher?"

I don't know why being a teacher impressed him, but I got the impression it did. I nodded. "Yes. I teach Grade Three. What do you do?"

He shoved his hands into the pockets of his hip-hugging jeans. "I'm starting at the hospital tomorrow as an orderly."

"Oh. That's nice." I offered a shy smile and tugged a piece of hair, wrapping it around my finger. His eyes captivated me, and under his attentive gaze, I felt like a nervous school girl.

We continued chatting until Lisa announced that everyone was heading out for coffee. Her gaze flitted between me and Joe. "Are you two coming?" I gave a small shrug and deferred to her brother. I still had lessons to finish for the following day, but when he said he'd go and arched his brow at me, I forgot all about them. Not since Greg had my heart fluttered like this, and Joe's attention flattered me. Although I spoke too fast, he was easy to talk with, and he seemed genuinely interested in me. I smiled and turned to Lisa. "Yes, I'd love to come."

Joe didn't have a car, so I offered him a lift. It wasn't far, but I was conscious of him sitting beside me. The scent of his after-shave filled the car and tickled my nose. After I parked and we walked to the coffee shop, he held the door open and stood back for me to enter first. His manners impressed me.

We ordered coffee and then joined Lisa and the others at a

long table. After she introduced him to everyone and he chatted with them briefly, he returned his focus to me. He wanted to know where I'd grown up, where I'd studied, and what I thought of Gladstone. When I asked him about himself, he told me he'd travelled around and had had different jobs, but that he was looking forward to starting this new phase in his life.

"A new start?"

He nodded and toyed with his coffee cup. "I recently gave my heart to the Lord. I knew my sisters went to church, so I came up here so they could help me grow."

I smiled. "That's wonderful. How did it happen?"

His gaze met mine and held. "Do you really want to know?"

"Yes! I love hearing how others met the Lord."

"Okay…" He paused, glancing down and fiddling with his hands before looking up and continuing. "I had a drug problem."

My brows shot up. "Drugs?" I'd never known anyone with a drug problem, and to be honest, I knew little about them, except that they were bad news.

He nodded and let out a heavy sigh. "Yep. I was an addict, but I've kicked the habit now, thanks to The Wayside Chapel and God."

"Right." I wanted to know more, but I was too scared to ask in case I revealed my ignorance. "Well, I'm sure your sisters will help you."

He smiled and glanced at Lisa, and then at their other sister, Linda. "Yes, being here will be good."

I studied him for a moment. My heart was going places I feared it shouldn't, and fast. I was attracted to him, but the mention of drugs alarmed me. But then, if he'd given his heart to the Lord and had kicked the habit, there shouldn't be a problem. I met his gaze and my heart fluttered again. His eyes were mesmerizing. A beautiful mix of blue, green, and hazel, enhanced by long, dark lashes.

When we left, his hand brushed mine. I don't know if it was on purpose or by accident, but either way, tingles ran through my body. We stood in front of my car, and he asked if I'd like to catch up during the week. I sensed this was another of those pivotal moments. It had been so long since I'd felt like this. I should have prayed about it, but before I had a chance to, I agreed.

He called me the next evening and we talked on the phone for hours. When he invited me to go for coffee the following evening, I offered to pick him up. We talked and laughed, and he made me forget about Greg. He was easy to talk with, and he treated me like a lady. He held the car door and pulled the chair out. Before I knew it, I was in love.

We started spending all of our spare time together. He loved his job—he was great with people and put them at ease. Quite the charmer, everyone loved him.

Joe was a natural athlete. He loved tennis and football, and watching him play was a pleasure. When he was younger, he'd represented his school in both sports and could have gone places if he'd chosen to. He also loved to dance, and whenever we went out, he held me tightly as we waltzed around the room. I was so glad I'd taken those ballroom dancing classes when I was still at school!

But despite attending church and Bible study, I soon discovered Joe was still battling addiction. I tried to ignore the signs and prayed that God would help him overcome. One night when we went out, he seemed different. I wasn't sure what it was, but the smell of alcohol hung on his breath and he was less than steady on his feet. When we sat at the table, I clasped my hands together in my lap and held his gaze. "Have you been drinking?" I hadn't meant to be so blunt; it just came out.

He reached across the table and looked at me with puppy dog eyes. I left my hands in my lap. "I'm sorry, Julie. I had a few after work."

I narrowed my eyes. "Seems like more than a few."

His shoulders slumped. "Yeah, maybe."

"Have you got a drinking problem?"

"No." His jaw tightened.

I was in unchartered waters. "Okay. Let's order." I left it at that, but after we'd eaten and were getting into the car, he asked me to drop him in town, not back at his sister's house.

I looked at him in dismay. I didn't know this Joe, agitated and edgy. "Why?"

"I'm not ready to go home, that's all." He leaned across the console and pulled me into his arms. "It's okay, Jules." He nuzzled my neck.

I pulled away. "No, it's not."

He let out a heavy sigh. "Something happened at work today."

My forehead creased. "What?" He hadn't said anything while we were having dinner.

"I watched a post-mortem."

I gulped. "Why didn't you tell me?"

He rubbed my arm. "I didn't want to spoil our meal."

"I guess that's a good enough reason. It must have been horrible." The very thought made me feel ill. My voice softened.

"Yes. I don't know how they do it."

"But why do you want to go to town?"

He ran his hand through his hair. "I can't get it out of my mind."

"And you want to drink?"

He nodded.

"Would you like to pray about it instead?"

"I don't know that it would help."

"It might."

He shrugged. "Okay."

I took his hand and bowed my head. "Lord, please help Joe to recover from this experience. It must have been terrible for him. Please fill his mind with good things and let him look to You and not use alcohol to get over it. In Jesus' precious name. Amen."

"Amen." Joe kept his head lowered. I sensed he was fighting an internal battle, and I prayed that with God's help, he wouldn't seek solace in a bottle. I'd seen the drunks around town, and I'd hate for him to join them.

I squeezed his hand. "Let me take you home."

He looked up and nodded. "Okay." His voice had steadied and I breathed a sigh of relief.

After dropping him off, I lifted him up in prayer again as I drove to my flat.

A few weeks later, I took Joe home to meet my parents. I hoped they'd like him, because we'd been talking about getting married. We shared the driving, but when we arrived in Brisbane, he wanted to stop at his auntie's house first. He was anxious about meeting my parents. I understood, because I was anxious as well. I hadn't told them he was aboriginal.

When we finally arrived, they were polite, but my Dad took me aside just before we left that Sunday afternoon to drive back to Gladstone. He told me in no uncertain words that he thought I was wasting myself by being with Joe. "He's a no-hoper. He's aboriginal, and he's got a drinking problem. Don't throw your life away."

Little did he know that his words only served to make me more committed to Joe. I wouldn't put him through what Greg's mother had put me through when she turned him against me. My dad didn't know about God's amazing grace and how He could change people's lives. My dad believed that a leopard never changes his spots. I believed in a God Who was in the business of doing just that.

When Joe proposed soon after, I accepted. I knew my parents wouldn't approve of us getting married, so we married in a registry office with only his sisters and a few friends to witness this pivotal moment in our lives.

It wasn't the wedding most girls dream of. I went to school that morning as usual, and when school ended, I hurried home to get changed. Not into a lovely wedding dress—I'd bought a new outfit, but it was just a dress you'd wear to someone else's wedding, not your own. As we said our vows and I became Mrs. Taylor, I gazed into Joe's eyes and asked God to bless our marriage.

We had a celebratory dinner with his family and our friends. An ache weighed on my heart, but I pushed it away. I'd married Joe without my parents' knowledge and against their wishes. I loved him, and they'd just have to accept that, whether they wanted to or not. I was an adult and could make my own decisions.

We didn't take a honeymoon. We had one night in the best hotel in town, and then we moved into a caravan we'd bought several weeks earlier.

Everything was fine to start with. Each day, we went to work and then came home. We took walks along the beach, Joe played tennis, and I started playing netball again. We went to church. He helped me with the I.S.C.F. group at school when he could. He loved the kids, and together, we planned to take them away for a weekend camp.

We borrowed tents and took a dozen kids into the country-side. We camped near a river, and they swam and ran around until they were worn out. Joe and I cooked, but we rostered the kids onto various jobs. We had a campfire at night with singing and games, and it was a wonderful weekend.

Joe wanted a family, and after several months of trying, I discovered I was pregnant. But my elation was tinged with concern. Joe had started drinking again. Not heavily, but one day when he didn't turn up after school to drive me home, my stomach churned with anxiety. It was in the days before mobile phones, and I had no way of contacting him. As we only had one car and we lived out of town, I had no choice but to wait for him. He finally arrived, three hours late and inebri-ated. I was furious and ordered him to get out of the driver's seat. I was tempted to drive off without him, but I didn't.

The whole way home he apologised and promised he wouldn't do it again. He kept his word—until the day my parents came to visit. They knew we were living together, but they didn't know we were married. They also didn't know about the baby. For weeks I'd agonised over how to break the news to them. When they said they'd come for a visit, Joe and I both knew the truth would have to come out. They'd be disappointed. Angry. But I hoped that hearing they were soon to become grandparents might soften their hearts.

As the day approached, we both grew more anxious. We tidied the caravan and bought new curtains and mats. Without actually saying it, we both wanted them to see that we were happy together and there was nothing to worry about. But Joe blew it. The pressure got to him, and he went on a drinking binge. I couldn't believe it. Of all days for this to happen, he chose the day my parents were coming.

I knew what had happened straight away. Lisa had told me not long after Joe and I married that not only had he suffered an addiction to drugs, he'd also had a problem with alcohol. I didn't say it, but I wondered why she hadn't given me that information before I fell in love with him. Would it have made a difference? Possibly. It might have made me think twice. She'd also said that I was good for him, and she doubted it would be a problem in the future, but I needed to be aware of the signs, just in case.

Great. The signs were everywhere. I raced into town and tried to find him. I didn't want to face my parents on my own. He liked playing pool, so I went to every pool hall I could find, but he wasn't at any of them. I went to every hotel in town. I was desperate. The longer the day dragged on, the heavier my heart grew. I wasn't going to find him and I'd have to face my parents without him.

Driving home in tears, I didn't want my parents to think

they'd been right about Joe, and have them tell me I'd made a mistake. I hadn't. We loved each other, and he was doing great. Most of the time. If only he hadn't panicked. But they'd see this as proof that they were right.

I pulled myself together. I had to put on a brave face. Pretend there wasn't a problem. Tell them Joe had been called away unexpectedly. But could I lie to my parents? I was a Christian, and Christians don't lie. But if I told them I didn't know where he was... *Oh God, please help me. Please bring Joe home in time... please help my parents understand.* A lump grew in the pit of my stomach. They'd be at the caravan park in less than an hour. I pulled the car up beside the caravan and climbed out. I prayed with all my heart that he'd be there, but I had no idea how Joe would have gotten home. There were no buses or public transport. Nevertheless, I held my breath as I opened the door and stepped inside. To my very great relief, he was there, sprawled on the bed, snoring.

CHAPTER 3

I shook Joe and tried to wake him. He reeked of stale alcohol. Anger swept through me and my hands trembled, but I had no time to let fly at him, so I took control of my emotions. "Joe, Mum and Dad will be here soon. Get up and have a shower. I'll make coffee."

He raised his head. His eyes flickered open but he quickly closed them again. He held his hand over his face, as if the light was too bright. I guessed his head hurt. I had little sympathy, but I pulled the curtain across, anyway. His eyes fluttered open. When he rolled over, he slowly swung his legs off the bed, rested his elbows on his knees, and hung his head.

I stood there with my arms crossed, glaring at him. How could he have done this? I glanced at my watch. We were running out of time. And then I heard a car pull up and stop outside the caravan. I quickly grabbed his shirt and dragged him into the shower. "Don't come out until you're sober."

He pulled my hand toward him as I turned to leave. Our

gazes met and held. "I'm…I'm sorry, Jules." His voice was weak, raspy. If my parents weren't outside, I'm not sure whether I would have slapped him or hugged him. Since they were, I pursed my lips and said, "Okay. Don't do it again."

When he closed the door, I pulled the curtain back and looked out the window and breathed a sigh of relief. It wasn't my parents—it was our new friends, Annette and Steve, who lived in the caravan next door. A moment later, Steve poked his head into the annexe and called out to Joe. He'd started doing this, and it annoyed me. He was a friendly chap, but there was something about him I didn't like. I couldn't put my finger on it, but he was a surfer with long blond hair, and though I didn't like to stereotype people, he seemed to be off with the fairies a lot of the time.

I hurried to the door and looked down at him. At least he hadn't come inside without being invited. I gave a curt smile. "Joe's in the shower, and my parents are coming. We'll have to catch up later. Sorry."

He got the message and left. I turned the kettle on and took two mugs from the shelf, placing two spoons of coffee into Joe's mug, and one into mine. Just as he turned off the shower, another car pulled up and stopped. I lifted the curtain. This time, it *was* my parents. I hurried to the bathroom to see if Joe had sobered any. Steam filled the tiny bathroom. Through it, I could see that his eyes were still etched in red, but he was passable. I hoped. He needed a shave, but there was no time. "They're here. Throw on some cologne and do your hair. Have you cleaned your teeth?"

"Yes."

I stepped closer and looked into his eyes. "Are you okay?"

My voice was softer than it had been before. We were in this together, and we needed to get through it.

His jaw tensed as he pulled a comb from his pocket and ran it through his hair. "I think so."

I blew out a breath. "Okay. Let's go greet them."

As expected, my parents were disappointed and shocked when we told them we were married, but to their credit, they didn't make a scene. In fact, after a while, when they heard about the baby and we assured them we were happy, they offered to give us a proper wedding.

I was so shocked I couldn't say anything to start with. I totally hadn't expected that. After I pulled myself together, I thanked them and said we'd have to think about it.

They stayed for several hours. They were just passing through on their way north, and although the afternoon had gone better than expected, I was relieved they weren't spending the night. Another time, perhaps.

Joe and I stood with our arms around each other and waved as my parents drove away. Once their car disappeared out of sight, he turned me to face him then pulled me close and kissed the top of my head. "I'm sorry, Julie. I really am."

I held onto him tightly and squeezed back tears as pain gripped my heart. I'd seen the hurt in my parents' eyes. I was a terrible daughter; they didn't deserve this. And yet, despite everything, they'd offered to give us a proper wedding. It was more than I could handle and I began to sob. Joe pulled me tighter and rubbed my back. "They're good people, your parents."

I nodded. "I know." Sniffing, I drew back and blew my nose.

He put his finger under my chin and tipped my face up.

Looking deep into my eyes, he asked, "Would you like a proper wedding?"

I drew a slow breath. To be honest, I hadn't really minded not having one. After all, it had been our choice, but maybe it would be nice to invite all of my friends from Sydney. Not Greg, obviously, but Sandy, Leigh, Brian, and the others. And to have it in a church and ask God's blessing on our marriage. I smiled, then nodded. "Yes, I…I think so."

He returned my smile. "Okay, let's do it."

"Really?" For some reason, I expected him not to want one.

He flicked some hair off my face, leaving his hand on my cheek. "If it's what you want."

Tears welled in my eyes. "I think so."

"And maybe we could have a proper honeymoon, too."

I smiled through my tears. "That would be nice."

I called my parents a few days later and told them we'd like to accept their offer. We discussed arrangements, and less than three months later, Joe and I had a proper church wedding with all the trimmings. My friends drove all the way from Sydney in a minibus, even though they knew I was already married. I was so happy to see them all, especially Sandy. She was my bridesmaid, along with my sister, Megan.

Joe and I went to Fraser Island for our honeymoon, the largest sand island in the world, just north of Brisbane. We enjoyed a week of sun and relaxation before returning to our life in Gladstone. I prayed that having our marriage blessed in a church would help us grow closer to each other and to God, and that Joe would have extra strength to stay off alcohol and drugs.

Not long after our wedding, Joe was offered a job labouring

at the new smelter not far from our caravan park. The pay was higher than his orderly's wages, so he took it. We were trying to save enough money to buy a house before the baby came, and every bit helped.

The smelter provided work for a lot of locals, but I soon discovered that alcohol and drugs were rife. Despite my prayers, I feared for Joe and wished he'd stayed working at the hospital. I was aware that being around others who drank and did drugs could harm his resolve to stay clean. I prayed harder.

He began visiting Steve and Annette more often, and each time he returned, he seemed different. One day, I followed him. An unfamiliar smell hung in the air as I entered their annexe. I poked my head cautiously inside the van. The three of them were seated around the table, and Joe held a funny looking plastic bottle in his hands. His eyes widened when he saw me and he quickly put it down.

I frowned. I didn't know what they were doing, but I soon learned that the plastic bottle was a bong and they were smoking dope. I felt like a fool. How had I not known? My only answer was that I'd lived a sheltered life and didn't know the signs. I didn't even know what it smelled like until that moment.

I made him come home, although Steve and Annette tried to get us both to stay. They even encouraged me to join them. I shook my head. "I'm sorry, I don't do drugs."

When we got inside our caravan, I sat Joe down and glared at him. "How long has this been going on?" I could barely control my anger and disappointment.

He hung his head and drew a slow breath.

My eyes narrowed and I stepped closer. "Joe. How long?"

He raised his head slowly and met my gaze. "A few months."

My eyes widened. "Is that where all our money's gone?" According to my calculations, we should have had a lot more saved by then, but I hadn't known where it was going.

"Sorry."

"Is that all you can say?" My voice didn't rise, but its intensity increased.

He shrugged helplessly.

I pursed my lips. "So much for saving for a house."

He reached for my hand. "I won't do it again, Jules. Trust me."

I stepped back. "You'd better not."

"I won't. I promise."

"I don't understand why you would do it."

"It's better than drinking."

I blew out a breath, my shoulders sagging. "I don't understand why you need either." I had to do some reading. I'd obviously been naive in thinking Joe could kick his addictions that easily, and I had to understand more about it, especially with the baby coming.

"Come here." He reached out his hand again and pulled me onto his lap. "I don't. I just need you and the baby." He nuzzled my neck.

"And God?" I straightened and searched his eyes.

He nodded. "Yes, and God."

I was relieved to hear that. I believed that as long as he was involving God, this problem would be sorted. I believed that God did answer prayer, despite Him not giving me Greg back. "What can I do to help?"

Joe traced his finger down my cheek. "Just be here for me, that's all I need."

"I *am* here. You know that."

"Yes, but sometimes the pull is too strong."

"That's when you need to pray. And tell me."

"I'll try."

"Do you need professional help?"

He shook his head. "No. I'll be okay. I can do this."

I studied him for a moment. I wanted to believe him. But could I? "Okay. But talk to me. Let me know if it's too hard and we'll do something. We can go for a drive, play tennis, catch up with your sisters. Something."

He pulled me tight and kissed my cheek. "Thanks, Jules. I love you."

"I love you, too." And I did. I truly did.

ALL WAS WELL for a few weeks—until he went on strike. He had no choice. He was part of the workers' union, and they were striking for better pay and conditions. The whole smelter shut down while negotiations took place.

With no work to go to, Joe went to the pub while I went to school. *All day, every day.* I was so angry. Yes, he was on strike, but he could have stayed home or done other things, like play sport or do voluntary work. He stayed out late at night and often didn't come home for days on end. Some days, I was so desperate and angry that I searched for him, traipsing from pub to pub until I found him. Occasionally, he was happy to see me and he introduced me to his mates as his "missus", but other times, he dragged me outside and told me in a drunken slur to go home. Each time, anguish squeezed my heart and tears streamed down my cheeks as I drove home alone.

When he did come home, drunk and reeking of alcohol and smoke, I pretended to be asleep. He sometimes woke me and pushed me around, even though I was carrying our baby. He wanted to know what I'd been doing. When he was drunk, he didn't trust me and accused me of seeing other men. He wouldn't believe that all I'd been doing was going to school and coming home.

I cried myself to sleep often. I didn't like this Joe. When he was drunk, he was a different person, and I began to fear for my life. But when he grew sober, he returned to his normal self. The one I liked. The one I loved. Each time, he promised not to drink again. But I knew he would. Without a job, and with me at work, he wasn't strong enough to withstand its hold on him. I didn't know what to do. I was embarrassed and kept to myself. He didn't like me talking to anyone about "us", saying it was none of their business. All I could do was pray.

One night, he started throwing things around in the caravan. When he grabbed a knife for no apparent reason and threatened me, I thought I was about to die. Although he had no grounds, he accused me of cheating on him. I didn't even dare look at anybody else, but he was fixated with the idea of me betraying him, and the only thing I could do was to tell him over and over how much I loved him. Only him. No one else. After breaking almost everything in the van that we owned, he fell asleep in a drunken stupor. I stayed awake most of the night, too stunned and sickened to sleep.

When he woke in the morning, he apologised and said he

didn't know what had come over him. I didn't know what to say, so I said nothing.

Being in the latter stages of pregnancy, I was concerned about the effect this chaos was having on the baby. Although the doctor assured me the baby was healthy, I knew my emotional state had to have an impact and I prayed constantly for protection for this innocent little baby who didn't deserve to be brought into my nightmare.

One night soon after this event, we had a barbecue with a group of friends from the park—Annette, Steve and a few others. Although they weren't close friends, I felt safer around other people, but since the night he almost attacked me, Joe had been more attentive and well-behaved and I dared to hope we'd turned a corner. Most of them were high on dope, as was Joe, but I'd discovered that he was much better behaved when he was high than when he was drunk, so for now, I put up with it.

We were having a good time with everyone, but then, all of a sudden, he turned to me and said he was going out with a couple of his mates. My insides cried and I pleaded with him to stay. I couldn't understand why he would want to go out. I knew what it meant... he would come home drunk. We were having a nice time together for once, and I could go into labour at any moment. He knew that. But the pull of the pub was greater than the need to be with me. Soon after, when he drove off and the tail lights of our car disappeared into the distance, intense sickness and desolation swept over me.

I returned to the caravan and fell onto the bed in a sobbing heap. I tried to pray, but didn't know what else to pray for. I must have fallen asleep, because, in the early hours of the morning, our phone rang, waking me. I answered it with dread. It was the police. Joe had been in a car accident, and although he was okay, the car was wrecked and he was being charged with drunk driving. They asked if I could collect him once he sobered. I told them I couldn't—I didn't have a car since he'd taken it. As I hung up the phone, heaviness weighed me down. How much more could I endure?

Somehow, I don't know how, he got home. I stiffened when the door opened and he staggered inside. Surely he wouldn't touch me again. He sat on the bed and pulled his boots off before lying beside me. The smell of alcohol mingled with anxiety made me feel sick. He put his arm over me and hugged me. "I'm sorry, Julie."

Tears streamed down my cheeks. I was struggling to forgive him after so many times.

Early the next morning, just as the first fingers of daylight reached the van, I went into labour. Because he'd wrecked it, we had no car. Joe said he'd get one of his mates to drive us to the hospital. I was already in so much pain, I didn't care who took us.

I was admitted, but soon after, Joe left me and went to court to face his drunk driving charge. My labour was short and he missed the birth of our beautiful little daughter. When he finally arrived, his eyes lit up, and as he cradled her lovingly in his arms, my hope was renewed that she would make a difference, not only to his life, but to our marriage.

We named her Katie. She had his eyes, long lashes, and olive skin. She was beautiful.

To my huge relief, Joe stopped drinking and going out, and for a while, we were happy.

CHAPTER 4

*J*oe's sobriety lasted three weeks. Even with a daughter he said he loved to bits, he was unable to stay away from the pub. I would have drowned in despair if it hadn't been for Katie. She kept me sane when he went out and left me alone with her. All babies are precious, but she was God's gift to me. She was the reason I got out of bed, why I ate, and why I had to stay strong.

Not caring whether Joe approved or not, I started attending a women's group at our church. I needed the company and encouragement of other Christian women, but they knew about him and his drinking, and told me I should leave him. They were probably right, but it was easier said than done. Joe had told me on several occasions that if I ever left, he'd come after me and my life wouldn't be worth living. On the other hand, when he was sober, he told me he couldn't live without me, and that I was the best thing that had happened to him.

He always apologised after a drinking episode and often

brought flowers and many times he'd cry. He knew what he was doing to me but couldn't help himself. I believed he loved me, and although I didn't love his behaviour when he was drunk, I loved him. The women didn't understand.

I started doing some serious soul searching and often took walks to the river to read, pray, and journal while Katie slept in her pram beside me. How had I gotten into this situation? I'd had a stable upbringing, I'd done well at school, I'd gone through Uni, and I had a good job. So, what was I doing living in a caravan with an irresponsible husband and a baby who didn't deserve to be in this situation?

It had been my fault. So desperate for someone to love me, I hadn't thought through clearly enough whether Joe was truly the right person to spend my life with before committing to him. Instead of looking to God to fill my need for love, I'd allowed myself to fall for someone I shouldn't have.

But God is a god of love and forgiveness. I'd messed up, and even though I didn't deserve a second chance, I knew that in His great mercy and grace, He would forgive me and help me through this. I needed His strength and wisdom, as I had none left of my own. I was empty, worn out and helpless. I needed Him to guide me. I had to grow stronger and not let Joe push me around. I had to take control of the situation, because if I didn't, I feared for my future, and possibly my life.

I started to read books on alcoholism, because I now knew that Joe was an alcoholic, even more than a drug addict. He still frightened me, especially when he was drunk, but slowly, I began to stand up for myself. I told him that unless he took steps to get himself sorted, I'd leave, regardless of his threats.

Depending on his mood, he either showed remorse or grew

agitated. It was hard to pick how he would respond, but it did have an impact on his behaviour. He started to make more of an effort to stay sober, but he started to smoke dope more often. He said he needed dope to help him stay off the booze. I was less than happy about it, but since the dope helped to calm him, I accepted it in the short term and our lives stabilised for a while.

That stability didn't last, and I'd had enough. One day, I packed up and left. I got on a bus with Katie, and we went to the only place I knew I could go…home to my parents. I hadn't called to let them know I was coming. I just arrived on their doorstep with their little granddaughter in my arms. They were surprised, but not really. They said they'd expected me to leave Joe at some point, and they welcomed us with open arms.

We'd never been a family that talked about important issues, and although I tried, I found it difficult to share with my parents how I was feeling. I felt like a failure, but I put on a facade. I wanted them to think I was okay, even though I was a mess. Katie and I couldn't stay there forever, and I felt sure that Joe would know where we'd gone. It worried me that he might carry out his threats. I didn't tell anyone about the night he'd threatened me with a knife—I was too ashamed to admit I'd made such a terrible hash of my life.

Although I enjoyed the safety of being with my parents, I began to miss Joe and started thinking I should give him another chance. He phoned several times and pleaded with me to come back. He promised he'd change and said he couldn't live without me. I decided to go back, but only on the condition that he *did* change. He said he would. My parents told me I was making a mistake, but they didn't understand that I truly did love him, and that I was committed to making our marriage work. I'd had the time out I needed, and I was looking forward to starting again.

For a few weeks he really did try, but with his mates continually asking him to go out with them, he and I both knew it would only be a matter of time before he gave in. We had to move, so we did.

We packed our meager belongings and moved to the city. Still a charming man, Joe found a job within a week. He worked hard and things looked up. We started going to church again, and he seemed to be coping with everything. However, because we had nothing, we needed more money than what he was earning. Katie was still very young and I wasn't ready to return to teaching, so we looked for options. Finding an advertisement for a position as house parents at a church-run home for children, we applied for the position, never expecting to get it. However, after several interviews, we were told we'd been successful. Surprised and slightly overwhelmed, we thanked God for His provision and prayed we'd be up to the task.

Managed by a church organisation, the group home was part of a complex of four similar houses. We were allocated six children, all with deep-seated emotional problems resulting from years of being shuffled from one foster family to the next. Our job was to provide a stable family environment for them while they waited for another foster family placement. Joe thrived. He'd come from a large family, and he loved playing games with the children and being their 'dad'.

Feeling stable and secure at last, I called on the skills and theory I'd learned at Uni and worked hard to provide a loving, caring environment for those kids. For almost a year, life was good. Joe went to work, the kids went to school, and Katie and I had most days to ourselves. Joe had the occasional slip-up, which we managed to cover. Alcohol wasn't allowed in the house at all.

But one night, after a hard day at work, he went out and got caught for drunk driving on the way home. We couldn't cover that up, and despite pleas and tears, we were asked to leave the group home. With heavy hearts, we moved into a house not far away, and started life on our own again.

All the progress we'd made was wasted. Joe took it badly and started going out drinking again. When he went to court to face his drunk driving charge, because it was his third offence, he was sentenced to weekend detentions in jail for six months. I was in shock, but I soon relished my weekends without him. When he was locked up and couldn't get into trouble, I could go to bed knowing he wouldn't be coming home drunk.

That soon back-fired. He took sick leave from work because he couldn't handle being in jail all weekend and then working all week. When he didn't go to work, he had all week to go out and drink before returning to jail on a Friday night.

He became more volatile and uncontrollable and I grew frightened of him again. He would often come home and throw things around and accuse me of going out with other guys while he was in jail. I knew I had to leave, *again*. Although I was terrified of what he might do, I packed up and moved into a flat with my sister.

Soon after, I discovered I was pregnant again. We'd planned

to have another baby when we were in the group home, but now that everything had changed again, I felt confused and alone. What could I do? I prayed about it, and there was only one thing to do—go back. When I told Joe about the baby, he was over-the-moon and once again promised he'd make every attempt to get himself sorted out, once and for all.

So, despite Megan and my parents telling me I was crazy, I went back. Joe began regular counselling sessions with our pastor, a caring man who seemed to have some insight into what was going on inside Joe. Our church family stood behind us and hope grew inside me that finally, Joe might beat his demons. He still had occasional binges, but they were less frequent, and he made new friends who didn't drink or smoke.

This lasted only a month. I couldn't believe it. He threw it all in and went back to his old ways. I was devastated, and after discussing the whole situation with our pastor, I decided that the only option was to make a clean break, although I was five months' pregnant. I didn't tell Joe. I knew if I did, he'd become violent and I mightn't get out alive, so, packing quickly, I left with Katie and drove all night back "home", to my friends in Sydney. I didn't think he'd follow. He didn't have any money, and anyone who knew where I'd gone promised they wouldn't tell.

I'd called Sandy and warned her we were coming. She was more than happy for us to stay with her, but her flat was tiny, and after a week, I knew I had to find somewhere larger. She connected me with another lady in a similar situation, and the two of us, plus our kids, moved into a house not far from Sandy's flat.

As my pregnancy progressed, I experienced mixed

emotions. One moment I felt relieved that I was safe, the next I felt I was a deserter. I stayed in contact with our pastor and Joe's family in Brisbane, so I knew what he was up to—no good. At least he didn't come after me. When my time came, I went into labour and gave birth to another beautiful baby girl —once again without Joe by my side. His genes were very strong, as this tiny baby girl also had his striking features. Love for her filled me and I thanked God for her and prayed blessings on her life.

I gave in and called Joe to tell him about our new daughter I'd named Lily. Before I rang, I knew what would happen, but I couldn't help it. I needed to see him. He came down by bus and we spent a week together. At just over two years of age, Katie was so excited to see her daddy, and it tore at my heart. It was a good week, and after he promised to sort himself out once and for all, I agreed to go home. We found yet another house to rent, and tried again to rebuild our life together.

For a while, he really did try, but he just couldn't do it. At my wits' end, I tried everything I could think of, but nothing worked. Joe couldn't seem to break his habits, although he knew he'd end up losing both me and the girls forever if he didn't.

As a last resort, our pastor suggested he go to a Drug and Alcohol Rehabilitation Centre. Joe reluctantly agreed to give it a go, so we packed up and travelled five hours south to a lovely part of the world, on the mid-north coast of New South Wales, where I hoped and prayed Joe would finally get sorted. This facility was unique in that families were encouraged to live there together. One catch—the patient had to stay there for a month on their own first, to allow time to adjust without the distractions of having their family around.

The accommodations were in old railway carriages which had been done up beautifully. The people there seemed to know what they were doing, and since the place was in the middle of nowhere, there was no way Joe could just go into town for a few hours.

The centre was near where I'd spent the first few years of my life. My parents had moved to the country not long after I was born, so I knew people in the area the girls and I could stay with. We had a lovely peaceful week in beautiful surroundings, without any worry about what Joe was doing. I prayed for him continually and trusted that God was using the counsellors to affect real change in Joe's life. We knew it would take a long time, but I was excited that he was being cared for by professionals.

At the end of the first week, I drove to the centre for our weekend visit. As soon as I stepped out of the car, I sensed something was amiss. He seemed agitated, but I put it down to the fact that he hadn't had a drink all week. However, he told me as soon as we were alone that he wouldn't stay unless they allowed me and the girls to stay, too.

"They won't let that happen, you know that."

"I'm not staying unless they do." The too familiar vein in the side of his neck pulsed.

I swallowed the despair in my throat. "The three weeks will go fast. Please don't do this." I reached out to him.

Two of the staff approached. They knew what was happening.

Joe's face darkened. He argued with them when they tried

to make him see sense. He wouldn't listen. He grew louder and abusive. I was concerned someone would get hurt.

I knew they wouldn't budge, even though it meant we'd have to leave without Joe getting the help he needed. Devastated, I'd hoped so much that this place would be the answer we needed.

Utter despair filled me. I was also anxious because I'd never heard Joe yell such abusive words so aggressively before, and I didn't know what would happen. He forced me into the car, and as we were leaving, one of the counsellors passed me a book. I quickly hid it under my leg. I didn't know what it was, but I sensed that if Joe found it in the mood he was in, my life wouldn't be worth living.

I managed a glance at it a little later without him noticing. The book was by James Dobson and was entitled "Love Must be Tough." I'd have to read it without Joe knowing, but I knew it would help me survive.

As we drove away, I didn't say a word. I was too upset. But we had to decide what to do as we couldn't just keep driving aimlessly. Joe eventually calmed down and stopped the car.

When we had the discussion about where we'd go, he said he knew he could sort himself out if he put his mind to it, but that he needed me with him. He couldn't handle being on his own, and said he'd almost gone crazy the past week without us. I thought this was a strange thing to say since he seemed to survive quite well without me most of the time, given that he spent most of his time at the pub or with his mates, but I didn't say anything about that.

Neither of us wanted to return to Brisbane—we knew it wouldn't work. So, we decided to drive and see where we ended. We drove south and arrived in Launceston, Tasmania, a week later. We had just enough money to put the car, ourselves, and the few possessions we had with us, on the boat between the mainland and Tassie, and so there we were, as far south as we could go, about to start on yet another chapter in our crazy mixed up lives.

CHAPTER 5

a rriving in a city with nowhere to live and no income apart from the Disability Pension Joe was receiving because of his alcoholism, we had no idea of where to start. Joe wasn't into praying over things, so I prayed quietly and asked God to provide a job and somewhere to live.

With only the car to sleep in, we contacted one of the local church's social welfare divisions. To our very great relief, they had one family unit available which we could have for a month. I sent up a prayer of thanks. With two young children, the prospect of being homeless had filled me with anxiety.

The unit, new, modern, and fresh, was the nicest place we'd ever lived in, and my confidence in God's provision grew. We now had a month for one of us to find a job and somewhere permanent to live. Once again, I asked God if He would provide for us.

Joe and I scoured the daily papers and visited the employment agencies. And there it was! An advertisement in the paper for a teacher at a Christian school. I made the call, secured an interview, and got the job, all within a couple of days! My heart soared. The school was in Deloraine, a small country town, a half-hour drive from the city of Launceston. I fell in love with the town immediately. It was how I imagined an old English village to be, with stone buildings and beautiful gardens. I could see myself living here, possibly forever.

The school was in an old monastery which had been partly modified. When we told the principal we were also looking for accommodation, he offered us some rooms in another part of the building. Although not ideal, it was a roof over our heads, and we were totally grateful.

Joe stayed home and cared for the girls while I worked. Knowing his habits and how easily he could slip back into them, I was anxious about this arrangement, but there was no option. We knew no one and child care wasn't affordable. He promised he'd do the right thing, and I had to trust him. I prayed that God would take care of my family while I worked next door.

Joe liked sleeping, and I soon discovered that the girls were often left to fend for themselves. Katie was a responsible three-year-old, but Lily, at eight months, was into everything. I began to fear for their safety. When he was awake, Joe played games with the girls and took them to the park, but he rarely did any housework, and I soon discovered what it was like to work full-time and then come home to a messy house where nothing had been done. He stayed off the drink, though, so I put up with everything else to keep the peace. Before long, he grew restless and started looking for a part-time job.

We'd made some friends by this time—a young couple with

two small children who went to the same church we'd started attending. I was surprised, but pleased, that Joe got along so well with them, and I was more than happy to develop the friendship further. Chrissy offered to look after our girls if, and when, Joe found a job, which he did within a few weeks.

After several months, the members of one of the local churches heard about our family living in the school building and offered us accommodation in their manse. It had been sitting empty for some time because they didn't have a minister, and they thought we might appreciate living in a proper house, especially with winter coming. We gladly accepted the offer and moved into it within days. We didn't have enough furniture to fill it, so it felt big, empty and cold, but the local people were generous, and before long, it started to feel like a real home.

Our future started to look promising, and we were glad that we'd ended up in this town that, until recently, we didn't even know existed.

Joe started to play tennis again, and for the first time in our rocky relationship, we were almost living a normal life. He still had the occasional binges, but he seemed to be controlling himself more, and he wasn't as jealous or possessive as he'd been earlier on. We even started talking about buying a house —something we'd not even dared to consider until then.

The countryside around Deloraine was beautiful. Mainly farming country, it was green and lush for most of the year, and in winter, snow covered the tops of the surrounding mountain ranges. While on playground duty, I gazed at those mountains and was filled with awe at their beauty and ruggedness. For the first time in many years, I felt at peace. I was teaching in a school where the children were not only eager to learn English, Mathematics, and Science, but also about God and His ways. I was growing in my faith, and I believed Joe was, too, and it warmed my heart and encouraged me no end.

I shouldn't have been surprised when this stability came to an end, but I was. I'd so hoped we'd turned a corner and that our life would remain normal. I longed for normal with my whole being. But the quietness of country life got to Joe. He missed the noise and anonymity of the city, and so, despite my pleas not to, he started going into Launceston. He usually took the car, and each time, icy fear twisted around my heart.

Some nights, when he finally arrived home, I wondered how he'd made it because he couldn't even stand straight. It seemed he'd forgotten about his stint in jail, but as there was no other way to get into town and back, he was prepared to risk it.

Some nights he didn't come home at all. I'd be on edge all night wondering if he was okay, or if he was lying on the side of the road somewhere. I constantly dreaded a knock on the door from the police. Worse still, when he did finally arrive, he started interrogating me again about where I'd been and what I'd done and with whom. He started pushing me around again when he came home drunk, and I thought, "here we go again".

One morning, when he was sober, he told me he'd met up with some other Indigenous people in town, and that's whom he'd been spending his time with.

Joe's upbringing had been mixed. His parents had tried to bring their kids up *white*, although they all knew they were *black*. When they mixed with their cousins and other family members, they often started drinking, and anti-white sentiments were rife. I knew a little about this, but I'd never fully understood. I knew they had their struggles, but I couldn't see why they didn't just get on with life.

Joe had tried to fit into *white* society, but his grudges came out when he was under the influence. He believed he'd been hard done by, but to be honest, I couldn't see how he'd been directly affected. I knew about the "Stolen Generation", the aboriginal children who'd been removed from their parents and placed into institutions in the hope they'd assimilate, but as far as I was concerned, that was in the past. The government was going out of their way to help improve life for Aborigines. There were so many grants and benefits available to them that white people couldn't access, so I really didn't see what the problem was.

We had two beautiful little girls, we were living in a lovely town, we both had jobs, and our prospects for the future were good. I couldn't understand why Joe had started drinking again, and why he was spending so much time with his new aboriginal friends.

One day, when he was sober, I spoke with him very seriously, and said that if he didn't sort himself out, I'd be leaving again, and this time, it'd be for good. I'd grown braver after reading the book I'd been given from the Drug & Alcohol Rehab place, and knew that if things were ever going to improve permanently, I had to be strong and stand my ground.

Despite my bravado, I was growing more anxious about the situation, especially because we were so far from home. Joe had also started taking Katie with him into town on occasions, heedless of my pleas not to. He said he wanted her to get in touch with "her people", and to learn about the aboriginal culture. He started telling both girls Dreamtime stories and that they were black. He even told them on occasions that I was the enemy since I was white, which infuriated me. How dare he tell them such things!

But how could I carry out my threat? I knew he'd let me go, but he wouldn't let the girls go, and I couldn't leave them. Since I had no real choice, I stayed. Somehow I managed to keep my private torment from my school days, but people started asking where Joe was. As he was now working for an aboriginal organisation in the city, I was able to cover his absence to a degree, and I tried to ignore their looks of pity.

At some stage during this time, I started to suspect he was seeing someone else. The main giveaway was when Katie told me, very innocently, that Daddy had a new friend. I managed to find enough courage to quiz him about it, and he admitted it right away. Obviously, she was aboriginal, and he told me he wanted to move in with her and take Katie. He didn't want to take Lily because she was too young, but he'd fight me for her when she was older.

"Over my dead body!" I'd never been so angry, and my shock yielded quickly to fury. I yelled and screamed, and for once, I attacked him. I laid into him verbally and physically, but it did no good. He just packed up and left, taking Katie with him.

I fell onto the floor and cried. Lily tried to comfort me. I pulled her close and sobbed uncontrollably. I called in sick the next day, and the one after that. And the one after that. Finally, I came out of my daze and decided I had to return to school. Without a car, I asked Chrissy if she could collect Lily and mind her. When she arrived at the door, she immediately knew something was desperately wrong. I told her everything. I didn't go to school that day, either.

She took me back to her place and cared for me. When I was able to talk sensibly without breaking down every minute, we tried to work out what could be done to get Katie back. Neither of us knew much about the family law court or restraining orders, so all we thought we could do at that time was try to find them. We were about to leave for town when Joe appeared on Chrissy's doorstep. My eyes popped. I thought he was gone forever. Katie ran into my arms and I burst into tears.

I learned that Joe's new lady friend had never intended for him to move in with her, especially with a young child. They'd had an argument, and he walked out. He knew he'd have to crawl to me, but I was so glad to see them back, I didn't make him crawl for long. We had a long talk and he said he was sorry for what he'd done to me. He realised that getting caught up in all the aboriginal issues hadn't been helpful. I wondered what would have happened if his lady friend hadn't tossed him out, but I was so relieved to have him and Katie home, I let it go.

His remorse seemed genuine, but we'd been there before. He said he needed help with his drinking problem, but didn't want to return to the Rehab Centre. He quit his job and started attending church again, and sought help from our friends who were more than happy to help in whatever way they could, but with no experience in this area, they could really only be his friend.

Things settled down for a while, but I knew it would only be a matter of time before it all fell apart again if we didn't find real help. This help came in the form of a friend of a friend who'd just returned from a year away at a Christian community in south-west Queensland. We learned that the centre had been established to give young people, and those not so young, time out from the pressures and temptations of city living, and to provide an opportunity for study, and counselling, if needed. It sounded perfect. We made some enquiries and lodged an application. Quickly accepted, we started making plans for the long trip north.

Mixed emotions filled me as our departure date approached. We'd made some great friends I was sorry to be leaving, but I was looking forward to finally getting help for Joe. However, on the night of the school's end of year concert, he once again got caught for drunk driving. I couldn't believe it.

The first I knew about it was when a policeman came in halfway through the concert and asked for me. I swallowed hard as a sense of foreboding grew within me.

"Your husband's been in an accident, Mrs. Taylor."

"You must be mistaken. Joe's here." I glanced around, trying to locate him. As far as I knew, he was in the audience, watching the concert.

"I'm sorry, it's definitely him."

Realising he wasn't joking, I went into a panic. *Joe was minding Lily.* "Is he okay? And what about my baby?" I was talking too fast and my heart raced.

"He's in the hospital, but he's okay. I don't know anything about a baby."

Icy fear clenched my stomach. "She would have been with him." I could barely speak. Images of Lily lying in a ditch on the side of the road, or worse still, trapped in the car, filled my mind.

"Come with me. We'll find her."

I hurried to the patrol car and climbed in. Fortunately, the hospital was only a short drive from the community hall. When the car stopped, I jumped out and ran inside, and there she was, uninjured and being entertained by the nurses while Joe was being attended to. A cry of relief broke from my lips as I ran to her. But my relief soon turned to anger. I couldn't believe Joe had risked Lily's life by having her in the car after he'd been drinking. He told me he'd just ducked out for a quick drink because the concert was long and boring. Because he'd been minding Lily, he took her with him.

"I only planned on having one or two drinks. Sorry, Jules." His puppy-dog eyes didn't work on me anymore, and I lashed out at him and then promptly burst into tears.

"How could you! I can't believe you did that!"

Joe couldn't remember how the accident happened, but I heard from the police that he'd taken a corner too quickly and lost control. He and Lily were lucky not to have any serious injuries. There was no way of hiding this incident, so it was timely that we were leaving within a few days. I couldn't face everyone's pity.

All of our dramas had shocked the people in this little town, but this last episode confirmed to me that it was time to go. Since the car was a wreck, we had to book flights instead of driving. Joe didn't attend court since the hearing wasn't scheduled for another month, and we couldn't hang around for that long. He could never return to Tasmania unless he was prepared to face court, but we had no option. As far as I was concerned, going to Cornerstone was the last chance for our marriage to survive and for Joe to get help.

CHAPTER 6

*a*s the plane soared over the lush, green Tasmanian countryside on its way north, I gazed down at what had been our home for almost a year. We could have been happy in Deloraine. We'd even found a house in the foothills of the mountains we'd considered buying. We'd made good friends. I had a job I enjoyed. My chest tightened and tears welled in my eyes.

But we'd been given another fresh start. Although I had little idea of what lay ahead, I hoped and prayed Cornerstone would be the answer to all my prayers. I longed for Joe to be better, and I knew we could be happy if he could only stop drinking and could completely give his heart to the Lord. I sensed it wasn't just a physical illness, but also a spiritual one, that ailed him. He had many issues he was struggling with, but despite everything, I believe he loved me, and I loved him. It wasn't a perfect love by any means, and it might have been dysfunctional, but we were a family.

After changing planes in Melbourne, we arrived in Brisbane four hours later and spent a few awkward days with my family. They weren't aware of everything that had taken place, but they knew enough. With Joe unsettled, I couldn't wait to get out to Cornerstone.

Finally, the day came and we caught a bus to the Cornerstone Community just outside of Dalby, a small country town in southern Queensland. For the entire five-hour bus trip, Joe was unable to sit still. I prayed silently that his spirit would calm and that his anxiety would lessen.

Arriving hot and bothered in the early afternoon, we were greeted by the friendliest group of people I'd ever met. I felt at ease straight away and prayed that Joe felt the same. Apart from the friendly people, my first impressions were of the white picket fence, the heat and the flies. After living in Tasmania, where the climate was much cooler, it was a shock to be back in the heat of a Queensland summer. The sun was unrelenting and I couldn't wait to get inside.

Since we were the only family there at the time, we were allocated a suite, consisting of two bedrooms, a lounge room, and a bathroom. All the other students were singles and shared dormitory type accommodations and bathrooms. We felt very privileged.

The ten other students and four staff all thought our girls were gorgeous and cute. I guess I was biased, but I thought the same. The other students were younger than us, but it didn't seem to matter, especially as we had our own area. Two of the staff members, Matt and Suzi, were a little older, and lived on campus, while the other two staff members, an elderly married couple, lived in a separate house. John and Ruth had been missionaries in several South Pacific islands for most of their lives but had also spent time in Aboriginal missions in the outback and held a special place in their hearts for Australia's indigenous people. From the moment we arrived, they took a very close interest in Joe and hope grew within me that he would receive the help he needed.

Our days were structured. We were rostered onto jobs of various descriptions around the place, such as meal preparation, cooking, cleaning and gardening, but we also had outside paid jobs which helped to cover the expenses. These ranged from working in the local cotton fields, which was hard work in the heat, to domestic cleaning. We did these jobs in the mornings, and then, after lunch, did our studies, which consisted of basic Bible studies, psychology and sociology lessons, and discussions. We explored modern day applications of Christianity and discussed the various pressures young people faced in society. Since all the students had come to Cornerstone needing time out from city living, most had issues in their lives that needed addressing, and these studies and discussions were designed to help in this regard.

As well as the formal study sessions, there were opportunities for casual discussions and one-on-one counselling sessions. These sessions weren't intended to be threatening, but were important in helping to address the various issues that had been the reason for each of the students coming to Cornerstone in the first place.

I was so thankful to be there and enjoyed the friendship and support of the staff, even though it was a challenge juggling work, studies and motherhood. Sometimes, unable to get to class, I caught up at night time. But it didn't matter—I loved living in a community.

To start with, Joe did, too. He performed his jobs, went to work and to class, he did his "homework", he chatted with everyone, and in general, he seemed happy. But he refused to open up in his one-on-one counselling sessions. It was like he was pretending he didn't have any problems and that everything was fine. Since we'd had to explain about ourselves in the application letter, stating the reasons why we wanted to come to Cornerstone, the staff knew about his problems, so the only real person he was fooling was himself, and we all knew it.

One day, completely out of the blue, he accused me of "looking" at Matt, the younger male staff member. With that one statement, my world crumbled once again and I knew that everything was about to change. Although he'd only said a few words and I vehemently denied *looking*, I knew Joe hadn't dealt with *any* of his issues and it wouldn't be long before he went off the rails again. The spark of hope I'd held for his recovery and for our marriage faded.

He began complaining about how regimented the centre was, how ridiculous it was that he wasn't allowed to go to town on his own, and how he didn't like eating with everyone else at meal time. He grew more jealous and possessive of me, and accused me of flirting with the male students and staff members.

Although it went against the rules, one day Joe stated he was going to town by himself. Intense sickness and desolation swept over me. It was starting all over again. I pleaded with him not to go, but I knew by the vein pulsing in his neck and the determined look in his eye that nothing would sway him.

As he disappeared down the road, I retreated to my room, sat on the bed, and poured my heart out to God. Why would Joe do this? He knew what the consequences would be. And why hadn't God stopped him? He was all powerful, and I knew it broke His heart as well, so why hadn't He intervened in some way? I didn't understand. Was Joe's heart so hard that even God couldn't get through to him?

I would have liked to stay sobbing on the bed, but I couldn't let Katie and Lily see me so upset. I pulled myself together for their sake and continued on as if nothing had happened, all the time praying silently for Joe, that his heart would soften and that he'd allow the Holy Spirit to work in his life and release him from his addictions and inner turmoil.

He didn't return for three days. Constantly on the watch for him, my stomach was sick with anxiety as I did my best to be strong for the girls. When he finally staggered home, unshaven, dishevelled, and reeking of alcohol, he was greeted with a strange quietness. Everyone knew where he'd gone and what he'd been up to, but no one knew what to say.

He didn't apologise or explain, and I trembled with fear when he dragged me inside our unit and closed the door. He was still intoxicated, and he immediately started pushing me around, accusing me of all sorts of things. Then he began throwing things. My heart pounded as I dodged flying books, ornaments and toys. I didn't know what had brought this on, but I understood there was a battle raging inside him, and I prayed for protection.

I took solace that others were nearby and that the girls weren't witnessing their father's drunken antics. Not long after, he collapsed onto the bed and fell asleep. Hot tears welled in my eyes as I gazed at my husband, snoring, oblivious of the anguish he'd caused me yet again. I took deep breaths, and little by little, my trembling hands steadied and I felt calm enough to face everyone.

While Joe slept, I met with Matt, Suzi, John and Ruth. Given what had taken place, we should have been given our marching orders, but they knew how desperate I was for Joe to receive help and that this was most likely the last chance for our marriage. They were so kind and sympathetic, and like me, they believed Joe was fighting an inner battle and was at a crisis point in his life. They were prepared to allow us to stay if he agreed to certain conditions. I was so grateful. I couldn't face another failure. Another forced departure. I prayed that when he woke and met with them, he'd see sense and would be prepared to meet their conditions.

When he stirred several hours later, his eyes were red and blurry and several days of straggly growth covered his face. His dark hair was unkempt, and he looked a mess. Despite the gamut of emotions assailing me, I held my calm, drawing strength from the books I'd been reading, the support of my fellow students and staff, and from God. Heart pounding, I stood at the end of the bed, fixed my gaze on his, and waited for him to speak. I didn't know how much he remembered of what he'd said or done, or what mood he was in. Whether he'd be apologetic, or if his anger was still aflame.

Moments passed. The faint aroma of roast beef wafted in the air. From Joe's gaunt appearance, I guessed he'd be hungry, but I doubted we'd be joining the others for dinner.

He eventually let out a deep sigh, almost a shudder, and hung his head.

I stood my ground. I wasn't going to him. To tell him it was okay. It *wasn't* okay. I waited. Slowly, he raised his head and tentatively met my gaze again. "Are they…are they throwing us out?"

I raised a brow. "What do you think?"

"Probably." His voice was raspy, resigned.

"They want to meet with you."

"Now?"

"When you're ready."

"I stuffed up, didn't I?"

"You could say that."

"I'm sorry, Jules. I don't know what came over me."

I drew a breath and pushed back my tears. I'd heard this so often, but nothing ever changed. Did I dare hope once again that this might be 'it'? What if I did, but he ruined it again? How many more times could I endure such disappointment? But what choice was there? Without hope, I may as well walk away. But he wouldn't let me walk with the girls… I sighed heavily. "Okay. You need to clean up, shower, shave. And eat. I'll go get some dinner—we can eat in here tonight. But then you need to talk to them. If you're truly sorry, they might give you another chance."

"Really?" His face brightened.

"Yes, but it will come with conditions."

"I don't know if I can do it."

I moved to the bed and perched on the edge. "You've got to try, Joe. Please. For our sake. Can you?" I didn't want to plead, but he couldn't give up. Not again.

"I don't know that I'm cut out for a place like this."

I fought tears as I listened to his words with rising dismay.

"They just want to help you, that's all. Will you give it another go? For us? Please?"

He reached his hand out to me and I went to him. He held me tight while I sobbed into his chest. "I'm so sorry, Julie. I want us to be happy. I'll give it one more try, okay?"

Relief washed over me. "Okay. Thank you."

After he'd cleaned up and eaten, we met with Matt, Suzi, John, and Ruth. When he apologised for his behaviour and said that he'd do his best to not let it happen again, a glimmer of hope returned, lifting me out of my despair.

They did their best to get him to discuss the underlying issues that had triggered this situation. Maybe he truly didn't know what was going on inside him, but he still seemed reluctant to talk. In the end, they told him if it happened again, we'd have to leave.

I guess this was better than being told to leave right then, but the glimmer of hope I held was thin. I couldn't understand why Joe wasn't grasping this opportunity with both hands. It seemed he truly didn't want to get sorted, despite what he said, because if he did, why wouldn't he open up, especially to John and Ruth who'd gone out of their way to help him? I felt I was bashing my head against a brick wall.

Over the following few days, I walked lightly, aware that anything could set him off again. He was a ticking time bomb, and I think we all knew it. He attended classes but didn't join in. He made us sit on our own at meal-times. He was jittery and troubled. Matt and Suzi offered to pray with him. He refused. The only person he spoke to at any length was John, but Joe's hand gestures and body language told me he was agitated and volatile.

Knowing what Joe could be like when he felt trapped, I grew increasingly concerned as the situation escalated. Although we were free to leave at any time, we had nowhere to go, and no money, and he knew that. So, he did the only thing he could do—he disappeared without a word.

I expected him to turn up again like he had previously, although I knew that when he did, we'd have to leave, and that distressed me immensely. But days passed, then weeks, and he didn't return. I didn't even hear from him. The constant stress of living with him had taken its toll on me, so, in some ways, I was relieved and I relaxed without him there, but I was also concerned about him.

One day I called his sisters, but they hadn't heard from him either. It seemed he'd just disappeared into thin air. But then one morning about a month after he left, he turned up on the doorstep, looking and smelling terrible. He cried, apologised profusely for failing me and the girls, and then collapsed at my feet. I put him to bed after giving him a wash, and he slept for two days.

When he recovered, he said little about where he'd been or what he'd done, but he said he was prepared to give it another go, and that he'd take counselling sessions with the staff to try to sort himself out if they were prepared to let him stay. I think he finally realised that they genuinely wanted to help him, and that this could be his last chance.

After further negotiations, and to my very great surprise, we were allowed to stay. Over the following weeks, to my great joy and relief, Joe kept his word and spent hours in private counselling sessions. I was over-the-moon. At last, he was opening up and seemed willing to let go of all the hurt from his childhood years which I'd been unaware of. He finally admitted he was an alcoholic and started going to Alcoholics Anonymous.

He was a new person, much happier and less troubled than before. For several weeks, he continued his counselling sessions and attended AA in town, and we fitted back into the Cornerstone routine. The other students were pleased he was sorting himself out as they'd been concerned about his treatment of me, and about his overall behaviour.

I started to believe that we were finally on the path to a normal life, when one day, totally unexpected, and for no apparent reason, he lost it. To this day I don't know what happened, but he started shouting at me and pushing me around, again. He then stated he was going into town and that I'd better be ready to leave when he returned.

I grew hysterical trying to stop him from walking out the door, but it didn't make any difference. He just left, but as he left, he turned and told me I could leave if I wanted, but I wasn't to take the girls. If I did, he'd hunt me down and kill me.

Something had snapped inside him because he'd been making great progress over the previous few weeks. I was in shock. Whilst he'd told me at various times before that if I wanted to leave him I could, but that if I did, I couldn't take the girls, he'd never actually threatened to kill me.

I didn't know what to do, but I couldn't go through it all again. I couldn't face leaving with him when he returned—we had nowhere to go, but more importantly, I was tired. I had no energy to start over somewhere else.

I was also scared and certainly not prepared to leave the girls behind. There was no way he'd be able to care for them on his own—he couldn't even look after himself. However, I took his threat seriously. I should have gone to the police and taken out a Domestic Violence Order against him, but they weren't that common back then, and even if I had one, I very much doubt he would have paid any attention to it and my life would still be in danger.

Hearing raised voices, Matt and Suzi came to see if I was all right. Since I was distraught, they knew right away I wasn't. I told them about Joe's threat and they agreed with me—it shouldn't be taken lightly, and a definite plan of action had to be worked out before he returned. They suggested that the students care for the girls while we discussed the options. My heart ached for my little girls. Although they didn't understand fully what was going on, they were aware that something bad had happened. How could Joe have done this again? All too familiar disappointment lodged in my stomach like a dead weight.

We went to John and Ruth's place. Matt and Suzi said we needed their input as they were out of their depth. I felt terrible. We'd put them all through so much over the time we'd been there, but I had no one else to turn to. They all knew the situation was out of control, and that whatever decision was made would result in emotional turmoil one way or the other. We discussed various options, but the only real one was that I had to leave and go somewhere safe with the girls. Staying and waiting for Joe to return wasn't an option. We all knew there'd be no choice but to leave with him, and I couldn't bring myself to go through all that again. I'd had enough. My will to keep going had left, and after his physical abuse and threats, I was more frightened of him than ever.

All five of us had difficulty coming to terms with the decision, as we all believed that marriage was for life, and so even suggesting that I leave him went against everything we believed. However, given the threats he'd made, and the physical danger that not only me but the girls were in, we came to accept that leaving was the only option. John and Ruth promised they'd try to work with him when he came back, if he allowed them to, with a view to eventual reconciliation, but they accepted that this might never happen.

And so, the plan of action formulated. John and Ruth suggested we go to the main Cornerstone complex in far north-west New South Wales. They thought Joe was unlikely to find us there, and if by some chance he did, the people there would know how to handle him. That seemed a better option than going home to my parents, the first place he'd think of, and I didn't want to put them in danger. As I couldn't think of anywhere else to go, I agreed with their suggestion—Cornerstone, Bourke.

CHAPTER 7

ot knowing how much time we had before Joe would be back—days, weeks, or hours, we assumed hours, just in case. Then started a mad rush to pack our gear for the long trip to Bourke. One of the staff members from Bourke Cornerstone was passing through later that afternoon on her way back from Brisbane. Leonie had room in her van for the three of us and agreed to take us with her.

Leaving was an emotional event. I'd made some great friends during the few months we'd been there, and many tears were shed as we said our good-byes. They all wished me well and promised to pray, but I was very aware that I wasn't just going to a new place, I was actually leaving Joe. Despite what he'd done to me, we'd been together for over five years. We'd been through so much, and I'd clung to the hope that one day he'd allow God to change him from the inside out, to give him a clean start, and that our marriage would survive. A sense of failure weighed heavily on me as the van pulled away. I waved until they were all mere specks in the distance.

I'd told the girls we were going on a long drive, but I had no idea how long. As the hours ticked by, I wondered whether I'd made the right decision. The road from Dalby to Bourke went straight west for three hours, then straight south for another six. The road, if you could call it that, was a narrow strip of bitumen full of pot-holes and rough edges. Whenever another car approached, both cars moved across into the dirt to pass safely. As dark approached, kangaroos darted across the road. By the number of carcasses on the side of the road, many didn't make it.

Sometime during the night, the bitumen ended and the road became a corrugated, red-dirt track. For the best part of an hour, the van bumped and skidded until Leonie finally slowed and turned into a complex of low lying buildings in the middle of nowhere. The girls had fallen asleep and had thankfully missed the worst of it. For most of the trip, I doubted we'd get there in one piece, although Leonie assured me she'd driven the road many a time and knew every corrugation and pot-hole.

Beds awaited us when we arrived, and as soon as I'd put the girls down, I collapsed into a fitful sleep. So much had happened in less than twenty-four hours and I had trouble coming to terms with it all. I couldn't help but wonder if Joe had returned, and if he had, what had eventuated. No doubt he would have been enraged.

The girls woke me the following morning when they climbed into bed with me. I held them tight and assured them we'd be okay here. We'd been given a small room in a block of six, but the bathroom was a communal one, so after a few moments, we got up, dressed, and then ventured outside. My eyes widened. Apart from a small patch of grass surrounding a house about a hundred yards away, red dirt covered the whole area. I'd never seen anything like it. Even Cornerstone at Dalby looked lush compared to this. With one arm around Katie, and Lily perched in my other and clinging to me, I drew a breath and walked down the steps and headed to the bathroom we'd used the night before.

Leonie had promised to introduce me to the other staff members over the communal breakfast. I was glad to see her when we emerged from the bathroom. Several other female students had given me a brief nod as we washed our hands, but I could tell from their puzzled expressions, they hadn't been told about us and must have wondered who we were. I was in no frame of mind to fill them in.

Leonie's warm smile encouraged me. I could have easily burst into tears. Never had I been in such an isolated, desolate place. She held her arms out and offered to take Lily from me, but Lily clung to me as tightly as a koala bear to its mother, so instead, she took Katie's hand.

"How did you sleep?"

"Not wonderfully."

"Come on then, we'll get some coffee."

I followed her into a large building which I soon learned was the hub of the centre. Rows of tables with bench seats on either side filled the dining area, and off to the side were smaller rooms where meetings and study sessions were held. People milled everywhere, some were lined up to get their breakfast from the counter, while others were already seated, eating and chatting in groups. It reminded me of the camps I went on as a teenager, and one camp in particular…the one where I'd met Greg. An ache tore through my heart. How had I gotten from that to this? It was almost inconceivable that my life had turned out as it had.

On the brink of a fresh wave of despair, I recalled the verse that Suzi had encouraged me to cling to whenever I felt this way… Jeremiah chapter 29, verse 11: *"For I know the plans I have for you," declares the Lord, "plans to prosper you and not to harm you, plans to give you hope and a future."* I took comfort from that and trusted that God, in His goodness, had something wonderful planned for me. That even though I'd messed up, it wasn't the end. I had hope of a future, a good future, and being here was the start.

The morning passed with meetings and settling in. I found everyone to be friendly and I soon appreciated that once again, God had provided a wonderful network of people to help and support me. As the centre was at capacity, and the room we'd slept in was somebody else's, we were offered the only accommodation that was available—a small, old caravan. Since Joe and I had started our married life in a caravan, it didn't overly concern me. It was a roof over our heads, and I was grateful.

When I met with the senior staff members that first morning, I shared with them a little of what had led to me being there. They were concerned about what would happen if Joe turned up unannounced. Although it was unlikely he would, given its remoteness, they suggested that neither the girls or I should ever be far away from the main area, at least until we felt the danger period had passed. As Cornerstone was on private property, they were fully prepared to call the police if he turned up. They had every right not to allow him entry. They also had a responsibility to the other students and didn't want to place them in danger.

A roster was to be worked out amongst the students and some of the staff to help with minding the girls so I could have some time to myself, to allow me to continue with some of the study sessions, and to do whatever jobs I could do to help pay my way. They also offered one-on-one counselling sessions to help me address and deal with everything that had happened and was likely to happen in the weeks and months ahead. I was now facing life as a single parent, although in reality, I'd already been raising the girls on my own for a long time. Joe had never taken his role as a father seriously, although he loved playing with the girls when he was sober.

Later, when I thought about everything I'd been through, I wept inconsolably. The years of inner torment following my breakup with Greg; the early days when Joe and I started dating; our secretive marriage that was doomed from the beginning; all the places we'd been, and the people we'd met who'd gone out of their way to help us. And the girls. How wrong it had been to think they might help change Joe and save our marriage. They deserved better. Much better.

During the weeks of personal confrontation, the loving care the staff showed me was no less than amazing. They cried with me, they listened to me, they prayed with me, and they challenged me. They challenged me to be strong, not in myself, but in God. I'd always believed in God, and I knew I was saved, but especially in the years following the breakup with Greg, I lacked the ability to truly trust Him. I'd held the belief that I'd never find anyone like Greg again, and so when Joe came along, in my loneliness, I allowed myself to fall for him.

If only I'd done things differently. I should have been strong enough to break up with Joe right at the start, but I hadn't, and now I was paying the price. But, *in all things, God works for the good of those who love him.* I had to trust that He would work this out for good. Somehow.

The girls and I settled into a routine, but thoughts of Joe were never far away. I constantly wondered where he was and what he was doing, and if he'd turn up one day out of the blue. And if he did, would he carry out his threat?

I'd heard from Leonie that he'd returned to the other campus two days after I left, drunk and dishevelled, demanding they tell him where I was. Because he refused to leave and was hostile and menacing, they called the police. He was taken away and locked up overnight, but he was let go the following morning after the Cornerstone staff said they wouldn't press charges—so long as he only came back when he was sober and was prepared to talk in a reasonable manner.

They told him that they knew where we'd gone but wouldn't tell him, and that if he ever tried to make trouble again they'd press charges. He said he didn't want anything more to do with Cornerstone, and that he'd find us without their help. They gave him some money and told him to go home to his family, which Leonie told me he did.

As the days and weeks passed, I dared to hope that we were safe from him and that he wouldn't come after us. But then, the unimaginable happened—I discovered I was pregnant again. Embarrassed, I kept it to myself for as long as I could. How had this happened? I'd been careful and taken precautions. Although Joe wanted another baby, I knew how irresponsible it would be under the circumstances. And then I remembered the night he flushed my pills down the toilet. I truly hadn't thought it would matter because I went out as soon as I could and got a new script which I hid from him. But obviously, it had. I felt ill, and not just from morning sickness.

Very slowly, I came to terms with the fact that I was carrying another baby, and that I'd be doing it on my own. *Again.* When I broke the news to the staff, they hid their surprise well but stated their concern for me, as I was still emotionally fragile. They went out of their way to help and support me.

Robyn, the wife of one of the staff members, minded the girls so I could take afternoon naps, and Leonie helped whenever I needed anything, but at night, when I was alone, my thoughts turned to Joe. I'd had no updates of his whereabouts and I wondered what he was doing, although I probably didn't have to guess too hard.

Despite the support of the staff and students, I still felt the burden of carrying my baby without the support of his or her father. Thankfully, my pregnancies were physically easy, although emotionally, they were a struggle.

I considered calling Joe's sisters to see if they'd heard from him, but then I told myself it was a stupid thing to do. I was still weak and vulnerable, and I knew how easy it would be to take him back if he apologised. We'd been there before...

So I stayed strong and didn't try to find him. For a while. Eventually, I succumbed, reasoning that he had the right to know I was pregnant, even though I knew how it would end.

I didn't tell anyone what I was about to do. After all the

support I'd been given, I felt disloyal, but I couldn't help it. I had to try to contact him. So, one night, I used the phone and called one of his sisters. He wasn't there, but she thought he was about somewhere and she'd try to find out. She told me to call back in a day or two. Although she asked, I kept my whereabouts secret. She understood why I didn't want to tell her.

When I called two days later, she told me she'd found him. As expected, he'd been drinking for weeks and was a right mess. When he heard that I'd called, she said he broke down and cried. If I wanted to speak to him, she told me to call back the next night and she'd try to get him sober enough to talk.

Confused thoughts and feelings bombarded me. As I hadn't told anyone I'd tried to find him, nor told his sister my whereabouts, I could have easily left it at that, but the thought kept nagging me that Joe had a right to know about the baby. Maybe it was hormones. Maybe it was loneliness. Maybe it was weakness. Whatever it was, I made the call.

My heart pounded as I waited for someone to pick up. When I heard his voice, tears welled in my eyes. It was his soft, gentle voice, the one I liked. Not the horrid, hateful one I detested and that sent shivers down my spine.

He broke down and wept when I told him I was expecting another baby, and he said how sorry he was, and how he couldn't live without me and the girls. If I could just give him one more chance, he'd show me that he could do it. I'd heard it all before.

I was determined not to tell him where I was. I was only calling to tell him about the baby.

"But Jules, I need you. I'm truly sorry. Please believe me." When he broke down again, my resolve weakened. I told him that if he wanted to see me and the girls again, he'd have to sort himself out on his own first. I couldn't go through it all again, and I wouldn't tell him where we were.

He kept asking, promising he'd change.

"No, you have to do it on your own first."

He eventually agreed to try, but asked me to call every day.

"No, I'll call once a week." I amazed myself at how strong I'd become. After I ended the call, I felt relieved that I'd talked to him, and a small glimmer of hope reappeared. Maybe me being strong would spur him to seek help on his own. I'd tried to show tough love in the past but had never succeeded for long, as he always managed to wear me down. I needed to stay strong this time, I really did.

I still didn't tell anyone I'd spoken with him, and so the weeks went by. Each week I called him as promised. Most times he was there. His sister told me he'd started going to church again and that he was meeting regularly with the local pastor. He'd also started attending AA. She thought he was doing well, and as far as she knew, he hadn't had a drink since the first night I'd called. But he'd done that before. He'd been able to stop drinking for months at a time, but then something would happen and he'd start again, so although I was hopeful, I was also sceptical.

The phone calls continued for a few more weeks, but Joe gradually wore me down and I ended up telling him where we were. As soon as the words left my mouth, I knew everything was about to change again. Annoyance at my weakness gnawed at my insides.

Joe said he'd catch a bus. I told him I had to talk to the

Cornerstone staff first. He reluctantly agreed to wait, and I hoped he'd keep his word.

I was nervous when I confessed to the staff that I'd been talking to Joe and that he wanted to come and visit. Their response surprised me. I totally expected to be reprimanded. Instead, they were happy to have Joe come for a visit, but on the condition that he abided by their rules. As soon as I conveyed this news to him, he booked a bus and was there within forty-eight hours.

The girls were so excited to see him, and he was ecstatic when they ran to him and jumped into his arms. As he twirled them around, tears sprang to my eyes. Despite his frequent absences, the girls had missed him; it had been so hard explaining to them why Daddy wasn't with us.

I studied him as he twirled the girls. He looked physically better; he'd put on some weight, which meant he must have been eating, and he was clean-shaven, and his hair had been recently cut. He'd made an effort.

When he held me in his arms and gazed into my eyes, he apologised and told me he loved me. How I wanted to believe him.

"It's only a visit, Joe. That's what we agreed to."

"I know. I'm just so happy to see you and the girls."

We were given time to ourselves, and after a few days, when it seemed he wouldn't cause any trouble, we were loaned one of the centre's cars so we could have a day out together. This was risky—I knew what he was like and that it was possible he'd been putting on an act all this time and that as soon as we were away from Cornerstone, he could suddenly change. But I gave him the benefit of the doubt and prayed for the best.

He behaved himself and we had a good day together as a family. We shared a picnic by the side of the Darling River, and Joe and the girls enjoyed their time playing together. He had been pushing to discuss what we were going to do, and I'd kept putting it off, but it seemed this was the right time to discuss it. I was hesitant to let him back into my life permanently, but he maintained that he really had changed. He was excited about the new baby, and he promised to do everything he could to make our relationship work.

I eventually agreed to let him stay, on the condition that he agreed to regular counselling, and that if he ever had a drink again, that would be it—absolutely, no way back. He acquiesced, and so when we returned to Cornerstone, we met with the staff and asked if he could stay, and if he could join in with the normal program. They talked with him for a long time about what would be required of him, and in the end, they consented to allowing him to stay, but only on the conditions I'd already laid out.

Accommodation at the centre was still tight, but the caravan the girls and I lived in wasn't big enough for four of us. The only option was another older, even smaller caravan. We spent hours clearing it of spiders and dirt, and eventually, it was livable. Joe and I moved into it, leaving the other caravan, which was parked right beside, for the girls. They thought it fun having a caravan to themselves.

I didn't know how it would pan out. There was every chance Joe would fall off the rails again, but it was a risk I had to take. I felt strongly that we needed this chance, despite his threats to kill me. I doubted I could have lived with myself had I not told him about the baby, so I had to trust he'd do the right thing, and that the girls and I would be safe.

Joe joined in with the work roster and studies and had his regular counselling sessions, and it all seemed to go well. During the counselling sessions, he opened up more than he'd ever done before, and he started to address the issues in his life that had caused him to not only drink, but to be afraid of commitment and responsibility. Deep down issues that had been a part of him for a long time. It was truly an answer to prayer that he finally had highly experienced and trained counsellors to help him address them.

After several weeks, they felt he'd do better living away from the community. I was immediately alarmed. I appreciated having other people around, not only for the fellowship and companionship, but also for safety. None of them had seen him at his worst, and even though he was doing well, I still carried images in my mind of all the times he'd attacked me.

They explained to me that for him to be truly free of his past, he needed to learn to be responsible for his family. He needed a proper job, and we needed a proper home, especially with another baby on the way. I was less than convinced, but I had little choice, and so arrangements were made for us to move into town, half an hour away, along a dry, red-dirt road.

CHAPTER 8

*W*e moved into a small house on the edge of town, all we could afford until Joe found a job, but after living in a tiny caravan, the house seemed like a mansion. Bourke, population two-thousand, half of whom were Indigenous, was not a pleasant town. Hot, flat, and dry, it bore no resemblance to Deloraine at all. Most shops had bars across the windows, and Indigenous youth roamed the town in gangs, especially at night.

I questioned the wisdom of moving away from the community. I doubted Joe was strong enough to withstand the pressure of living in a town that had more pubs than churches, but the Cornerstone staff truly believed it was the right thing to do. There was no choice but to trust their judgment.

They agreed to continue meeting with Joe on a weekly basis and were prepared to help us out in whatever way they could, including financially, until he found employment. They wouldn't leave us on our own, and for that I was grateful.

Using the Cornerstone connections, Joe soon secured a position with the local radio station doing odd jobs. It was a start, and he seemed to enjoy it. Although intelligent, because of his problem with drink and drugs, he didn't have any qualifications, and consequently, he could only do odd jobs and labouring.

After living in a community, surrounded by others, I found living in town to be lonely, especially when Joe started work. Robyn and Leonie dropped in when they came to town, and I eagerly awaited their visits. Robyn encouraged me to join a mother's group run by one of the local churches, which I did, and I also started attending a Bible study group each week.

I made some friends, one of whom became close. Sue's parents owned the property Cornerstone was on, and her husband, Chris, was a manager at the local radio station. They had six children, and Sue and I connected immediately. She encouraged me to visit whenever I wanted, and so the girls and I spent a lot of time at her house. Joe wasn't fond of Chris. I'm not sure why, but thankfully, he didn't mind me spending time with Sue.

Without air-conditioning in our tiny house, I struggled physically in the heat. The girls cooled off in a small, plastic blow-up pool, but since we could only fill it with brown bore water, it looked like they were swimming in mud. It was better than nothing, and I sometimes joined them, although the water was tepid and murky.

Joe and I soon decided to look for another house. With my pregnancy progressing, I needed air-conditioning. We found one that was much larger and moved within days. I started to think that the staff had made the right call. Joe enjoyed his job, we had a decent house, and we were going to a church we were both happy with. I so loved standing beside Joe and hearing him sing worship songs and hymns. It thrilled my heart and soul after all this time. The Cornerstone staff kept their word and maintained their meetings with him, and provided any support we needed. He even started playing tennis again.

One of the things that had attracted me to Joe in the first place was his ability to chat with anyone about anything. This quality was the reason he was offered a trainee disk jockey position at the local community radio station. He was so excited. Chris, Sue's husband, had recommended him for the position, and so Joe's opinion of him quickly changed.

He was required to attend a two-week training course in Melbourne, and so arrangements were made for him to go. I was almost due and concerned that once again Joe would miss the birth. My doctor was concerned about the baby being too small and wanted me to go full term, but I was hoping the baby would come early so Joe could be there.

The baby didn't come early, not even on time. The doctor held off inducing me for ten days, the day Joe was due to leave for Melbourne. I couldn't persuade the doctor to induce me before then—he wanted to give the baby the best chance possible, and so, as Joe left for Melbourne, I went to hospital. I couldn't believe it. Joe didn't have a choice—if he wanted the job, he had to go on the course. There was no way around it.

After a slow start and a long labour, I gave birth to another healthy baby girl. She looked just like her sisters, and just like Joe. Whilst Elisha was small, she was perfect. I felt blessed to have another beautiful daughter. When Joe heard the news, he was ecstatic and wanted to return right away. He obviously couldn't do this since he'd just arrived, but I said the time would go quickly enough and that he needed to focus on the training.

Sue was minding Katie and Lily while I was in hospital. The doctor, aware of some of my history, thought a longer break would do me good and suggested I stay in hospital an extra few days, even though Elisha was thriving. The ward was quiet, and Sue didn't mind, so, I stayed. I had a wonderful week. It was a small country hospital, and the nurses were friendly and helpful. I spent quality time with Elisha and had plenty of rest, which was great since I knew how busy I'd be when I went home.

Before I knew it, I was back home with my three little girls. As Joe wasn't due back for another week, my mum and brother came for a visit and to help me until Joe returned. It was wonderful seeing them again, and I certainly appreciated the help.

Joe enjoyed the course and was keen to start in his new job. Everything was sorted, and we could now get on with our life. I couldn't believe that at last, we were living as a normal family.

I held one reservation about the job—Joe would once again be involved with indigenous issues. After our experiences in Tasmania when he went off the rails, I was concerned it could happen again. Before he took the job, I'd spoken with him about my concerns. He'd assured me I had nothing to worry about. He'd dealt with all of those issues, and he wouldn't let himself get led astray again. I had no option but to trust him, however, I prayed continually for him.

Part of his job was to interview local indigenous people on

a wide range of topics. This involved going into their homes and chatting with them before interviewing them. He met a lot of people and gained a reputation as an easy-to-talk-to type of guy. However, he was always being invited to the pub for a drink—a normal thing to do, but not for an alcoholic. For a while, he resisted, but the pressure was too great, and he eventually went. He said the locals would think he was snubbing them if he didn't. He told me he'd go, but he'd only have a soft drink. Despite my prayers, I had this horrible, sinking feeling he might not be strong enough to resist alcohol.

When he left, I prayed with all my heart that he wouldn't give in. We both knew he couldn't have just one drink. He was an alcoholic, and he hadn't had a drink for months, and this would be a huge test. To my great surprise and delight, he came home a few hours later—sober. It had been hard, but he kept his word.

He told me he played a few games of pool while he was there— a game he loved, and said he'd like to go once a week to socialise and to play pool. I wasn't happy. I didn't know how strong he'd be if he was continually surrounded by alcohol. I tried to discourage him, but he promised me it would be okay. Unconvinced, I couldn't stop him.

It was the thin edge of the wedge, and my worst fears eventuated. Joe got back on the grog. The first night he drank, he came home rolling drunk. When he woke the next morning, he barely said a word. He must have felt ill and possibly ashamed. I don't know, because he got up, dressed and left. I didn't try to stop him. It was no use. I'd been through it all before, so I let him go, but nauseating despair seeped through my body.

He didn't return until the following morning. I'd barely

slept as the dull ache of foreboding weighed heavily on my mind and heart. I wasn't prepared to go through it all again. But could I follow through with my threat to leave? I'd prayed all night, seeking guidance and strength, but in the clear light of day, I was hesitant to have it out with him. He was still inebriated and I knew how volatile he could be in that state. I remained quiet as he collapsed onto the couch. Too quiet, it seemed. He must have wondered why I wasn't angry, because he soon sat up and began questioning me about why I hadn't said anything.

He caught me off guard. I had to think quickly, sensing he'd recalled my threat to leave if he ever drank again. "There's… there's nothing to say. That's all. It's no use me being angry." I could hear the anxiety in my voice, and my heart raced as he approached and glared at me. The vein in his neck pulsed, and his breath stank. I recoiled from him.

"If you're thinking of leaving, forget it." His voice was slurred and he had that look on his face—the horrible one that showed itself when he was out of control, as if something evil had taken over inside him. He pushed me against the wall before staggering off to bed.

Although they were hiding, Katie and Lily had witnessed this attack. I went to them and held them tight, assuring them it would be all right. "Daddy's not feeling too good. How about we go to Sue's for a while?" They nodded eagerly.

When we arrived at Sue's soon after, she immediately knew something bad had happened and ushered me inside and made coffee. Defeat and despair assailed me. Joe had been making great progress, but now I was facing the reality that he probably would never change. He'd had so many opportunities, and so many people had gone out of their way to help him, but underneath, something stopped him from doing the right thing. If having three little girls to come home to hadn't helped, I doubted anything ever would.

Sue suggested I hang in there a while longer, to see if it was a temporary lapse. I didn't think it was, but after a lot of discussion, she asked if I felt in my heart that I'd done everything possible to help him, and whether I could look myself in the mirror and not feel guilty if I left and took the girls away from him. In the end, I agreed to hang in there for another week, to see if it was just a lapse, or whether he really was back on the grog.

She said for me to behave as normally as possible, and not become angry or aggressive if he said he was going out, just give him space to see what he'd do if he felt he was free to make his own choices. This would be hard, but I said I'd try, as maybe I did need to be absolutely sure, so that if I did end up leaving, I'd never be tempted to return or take him back.

She then asked if I'd mind her updating her parents at Cornerstone with the latest developments. Jack and Sarah had been interested and supportive of our situation right from the beginning, and she thought it might be helpful to have their input as well, given the seriousness of the situation. She'd also ask them all to pray for us over the coming week. I agreed. Everyone associated with Cornerstone was genuine in their concern, and I knew they'd be almost as disappointed as I was that it had come to this.

'What will you do if it's not a lapse?"

I shook my head. "I don't know. I really don't know."

"Leave it with me. I'll see if I can come up with some options."

Tears sprang to my eyes as Sue hugged me. We prayed and then I returned home. I needed to be there when Joe woke.

Wondering what the next few days would hold, I kept busy for the rest of the day with housework and playing with the girls. When Joe woke, I remained quiet, and when he said he was going out, I let him go.

The girls ate dinner, and then I put them to bed. They asked where Daddy was—I just told them he'd gone out. I watched a mindless programme on television to get my mind off the situation. I finally went to bed, but unable to sleep, I got up again.

Elisha needed another feed, so I fed and cuddled her, and promptly began sobbing. I didn't know if I could control my anger and disappointment if Joe walked through the door, so I decided the best thing would be to go to bed and at least pretend to be asleep if he came home, although I knew he'd most likely wake me.

I must have been more tired than I thought because I fell asleep. A loud thump on the front door woke me in the wee hours of the morning. My heart pounded. I took some deep breaths and got up. I opened the door slowly, and there he was, slumped against it, barely conscious, with a beer in his hand. I was tempted to leave him there, but he somehow realised I stood in front of him, and in a very slurred voice, asked me to help him in.

I managed to get him inside and into bed, and he promptly fell asleep. Although relieved he hadn't been alert enough to say much or to be aggressive, I dreaded the morning. He slept fitfully, and finally woke mid-morning. I hadn't tried to wake him to go to work as I thought the longer he had to sleep it off, the less aggressive he might be. I tried my hardest not to say anything to stir him and started talking as if nothing had happened.

The most difficult thing was that we'd just been offered another house to rent. One of the local pastors was going overseas for twelve months, and someone had suggested to him that we might like to rent his house while he and his family were away. It was a much nicer house than the one we were living in, and we'd accepted the offer a couple of weeks earlier. Moving day was scheduled for the following week. I wondered what we should do, but I didn't want to alert Joe to the possibility of me leaving, so I talked to him as if it was going ahead normally. He said he'd ask a few of his mates to help with the furniture, and that he'd ask for the day off work. He took a shower and then left for work—late. I was very relieved he hadn't been aggressive, but he hadn't apologised about the state he'd come home in, and in fact, he didn't mention it at all. It was like it had never happened.

The next few days followed much the same pattern, except that one night he didn't come home at all, and another night I got a call from the police saying they had him in the watchhouse and to come and collect him if I could. Apparently, he'd been causing a disturbance at the pub, and then had been wandering the streets yelling abuse at everyone he came across. They said they wouldn't charge him this time, but if it happened again, he'd be charged with causing a public nuisance and being drunk in public.

I struggled to keep my calm. How could I collect him when the girls were asleep in bed? The police were apologetic and said they'd keep him until the morning, but to come as early as I could. I got there at six a.m. He was calm until we got in the car, and then the abuse started as soon as we were out of earshot of the station. He was angry that I hadn't collected him earlier, and then he accused me of being with someone else and that was why I hadn't come. Not, "I'm very sorry for causing you this trouble", or anything like that. *I* was the one in trouble. I didn't get it, but then again, I'd been through it all before, and I was tired of it. The week was almost up—I knew what my decision would be.

He went to work, late again, and I went to visit Sue. She knew how the week had gone, and so it was no surprise to her when I said I couldn't take it any longer, and that I was convinced in my own heart I'd done everything I could. For the girls' sake, and my own, the time had come. I had to go. The question was, where, and how?

CHAPTER 9

*a*s promised, Sue spoke to her parents, Jack and Sarah, highly-respected, hard-working farmers who'd given part of their land to the Cornerstone community. She told me that if I decided to leave, they wanted to help. I was so over-whelmed, I burst into tears. She gave me a big hug, a tissue and a coffee, then called them again to tell them my decision.

Jack had planned to visit town that afternoon and said he'd drop into Sue's to discuss my options. I stayed there for the rest of the day with the girls until he arrived in the mid-afternoon.

I burst into tears again when he arrived. Sue's dad was the kindest, gentlest man I'd ever known, with a heart not only for the land but for people and for God. He and Sarah had seen the pain and anguish that Joe had inflicted, and although they'd hoped he would allow God to change his heart and his life, they realised, like everybody else, that Joe was shunning Him and real change was unlikely to happen any time soon. The most important thing now was for the girls and me to leave safely.

We sat at Sue's large kitchen table. She made coffee while I tried to settle myself. This wasn't the time for weakness, but since making my decision, my stomach had been clenched tight as I realised I was facing another pivotal moment in my life.

Jack sipped his coffee then met my gaze. "I'm sorry it's come to this, Julie, but Sarah and I are happy to help in whatever way we can."

I swallowed hard. "Thank you. I appreciate that."

"Sue said that you can't tell Joe you're leaving," Jack said, his voice, soft, caring.

I nodded and let out a heavy sigh. "I'd be worried what he'd do, and he won't let me take the girls."

"That's what I'd heard. I know you've left before, but do you think this is the last time?"

I knew everyone thought I'd been weak in allowing Joe back into my life so many times. And maybe I had been, but they didn't know the hold he had on me and my desperate desire to see him overcome his addiction. But I truly believed that I'd done everything I possibly could, and that this time there would be no coming back.

Drawing a breath, I squeezed my hands together in my lap. Verbalising my thoughts and emotions to Sue's father made it all the more real. If he and Sarah were prepared to help me leave, it would be so much harder to ever consider going back, even if I wanted to. I had to be one-hundred percent sure. But was I? Was I truly prepared to leave Joe forever? Would I be strong enough to stay away if he tried to crawl back again? I prayed I would be.

Straightening, I met Jack's gaze. "I think I've done everything I can. Joe's had every opportunity to get sorted and there's nothing more I can do." Tears welled in the corners of my eyes. "It grieves me so much. I really thought God would heal him, and I feel like I've failed, but yes, this is the end of the road. I won't be going back." My voice faltered but I rigidly held my tears in check.

Jack's mouth curved with understanding as his crystal blue eyes settled on mine. "Julie, you're not the one leaving. Joe's already left. His actions have shown that he's not part of your family."

As the truth of that statement dawned on me, a weight lifted from my shoulders, freeing me from the burden of responsibility I'd felt for so many years for fixing Joe. He didn't want to be fixed. He'd left me years ago. Maybe not physically, but he'd chosen his mates over his family. He'd spent money on alcohol and drugs instead of food for his kids. He'd left us to fend for ourselves. I could now leave without guilt because I wasn't the one leaving. How freeing that realisation was! There was no way I would go back this time. This was it. With Jack and Sarah's help, I could do this. Fresh energy filled me.

In preparation for this moment, Jack and Sarah had discussed my options with the Cornerstone staff. They had a place in mind we could possibly go, but now that I'd definitely decided to leave, they needed to confirm it. He told me he'd get back to me later that afternoon or in the morning. "We'll sort this out, Julie. We've got your best interest at heart, and we have connections. We just need a little time to work through the details."

I could barely speak as I thanked him. I had no idea what he had in mind, but I trusted him and thanked God for bringing people like this into my life. I was so blessed.

When he left, I hugged Sue and tears found their way down my cheeks. I had so much to thank her for, too—her friendship had meant so much to me during the time we'd lived in town, and now her parents were helping me to escape this horrid situation of my own making. I didn't deserve all this kindness, but I was immensely grateful for it.

True to his word, Jack called later that afternoon. Fortunately, Joe wasn't home. He told me that one of the past students from Cornerstone came from a farm in Western Australia, and that her parents had also run a children's holiday camp on the property. After making some enquiries, he'd learned that the building used to accommodate the kids was empty. He then called the girl's parents and told them about my situation, and asked if they'd be prepared to have me and the three girls stay there for a while. They agreed to help, and I now had a place to go to…on the other side of Australia, about as far away from Joe as I could get.

The next step was to work out how we'd get there. Jack said that he and Sarah would come into town the following day, and for me to meet them at Sue's place to discuss the details. A spark of excitement ignited within me, but I had to keep this from Joe. If he knew what was going on, I'd be dead.

That night, after the girls were in bed, I opened my Bible, seeking comfort and guidance. Joe hadn't come home after work, and I prayed that he'd stay away. Before I'd left Sue's place that afternoon, she'd given me a list of Bible verses to read, and they were exactly what I needed. Confidence that I would be safe grew within me as I read each one in turn:

'My presence will go with you, and I will give you rest.'

'Be strong and bold, have no fear or dread, because it is the Lord your God who goes before you.'

'He will be with you. He will not fail you or forsake you. Do not fear or be dismayed.'

'And the God of all grace, who called you to His eternal glory in Christ, after you have suffered a little while, will Himself restore you and make you strong, firm and steadfast.'

'My grace is sufficient for you, for My power is made perfect in weakness.'

Joe staggered in after I was in bed, but thankfully, he didn't make a fuss. The following day he got up and went to work, allowing me to go to Sue's without having to make excuses. I sensed that God was already looking after me because Joe's behaviour was so unusual.

Jack and Sarah had been busy. They had a plan worked out but the timing still needed to be finalised. I explained to them the dilemma of moving houses, due to happen the following day. I also told them of Joe's plans to play in a tennis tournament on Sunday in Brewarrina, a small town an hour's drive east, and that he'd be gone the whole day. He was going with his Monday night tennis team, and I was reasonably confident he'd go, even if he'd been drinking the night before. Somehow, he always seemed to get himself together for tennis.

With all of this in mind, Jack and Sarah suggested we still go ahead with the move. Not doing so could make Joe aware that something was afoot. Jack promised he'd explain to the owner of the new house, whom he knew, what had taken place once I'd left, and sort anything out with him that needed sorting, including money, if need be.

Overwhelmed by this kindness, tears stung my eyes and threatened to fall. Sue gave me a hug and a tissue. She knew me so well.

Jack suggested that while I unpacked after the move, I use the opportunity to repack, as it would be less noticeable. He said to pack only one bag for each of us to make it manageable. I should then pack the things I wanted to keep and store them in Sue and Chris's locked garage. They could stay there for however long was needed. Everything else I would have to leave behind forever.

I was to be ready to leave soon after Joe left for his tennis tournament on Sunday. The plan was for me to pack the car, an old Holden station wagon, with the girls and our bags, and drive to Cobar, another town a one-and-a-half-hour drive south of Bourke. Jack would give me directions to a property owned by one of his and Sarah's friends, and I was to leave the car there. Their friend would then drive us to the bus stop, where we'd catch the bus to Adelaide, via Broken Hill, a twelve-hour trip. We'd be met at Adelaide airport late that night by more friends, who'd take us to their place in the Adelaide Hills for the night, and then drive us to the airport the next morning, where we'd catch a plane to Perth. We'd then be met by yet another friend of a friend, who'd drive us two hours south to the farm where we could stay as long as needed.

My mind whirled. It was like an escape plan you'd see at the movies. My first comment to Jack, though, was that I didn't have the money to pay for it all. I had no idea how much it would cost, but I knew it would be a lot more than I had.

"Don't worry about the money, Julie. It's being looked after by some of the Cornerstone people and Sarah and myself. We all want to help you and the girls get to safety and have a fresh start."

Unable to contain my tears this time, they streamed down my cheeks. I was so humbled and felt overwhelmed by all the love and care shown to me by these special people. The thought of travelling to the other side of the country with three little girls was daunting, but I knew that somehow or other, I'd do it, especially since they'd worked out all the details for me.

Before Jack and Sarah left, they promised to write down all the details and contacts, but they wouldn't give the paper to me until Sunday so that Joe could not get hold of it. My job was to go home and finish packing, move house, start repacking, and then be ready to leave on Sunday morning.

After they left, Sue and I had a good long talk. She told me how much support I had at Cornerstone, as everyone had either seen or heard all that we'd been through over the years, and that although helping to break up a marriage certainly wouldn't be the normal thing for them to participate in, they felt that in this situation, it was the right thing.

They could see absolutely no future for Joe and me. Even though he'd been able to stay sober for a while, despite all of the help he'd been given over the years, it had never lasted. It was apparent that he didn't want to stop drinking and that he had no understanding of what it meant to be a husband and a father. As well as that, he wasn't a happy drunk and often became violent, so there was real danger for both me and the girls if we stayed.

I finally went home to finish packing. I didn't say anything to the girls about the plans—not that Lily or Elisha would understand—they were too little, but I didn't want Katie to be worried. I tried my best to pretend that everything was okay, although it was impossible to steady my erratic pulse.

Since we didn't own a lot, packing didn't take long, but the house needed cleaning, so I got busy with that to keep my mind off what was about to happen. I had no idea when Joe would come home, or even if he would. I hoped that he'd remember we were moving and that he'd actually show up with his mates to assist. There was no way I could do it on my own.

He turned up in a bad way just before midnight. As usual, he staggered in, reeking of alcohol and stale cigarette smoke. I helped him inside and got him undressed and into bed. He started thrashing around, and I prayed he wouldn't hurt me. I could certainly do without that. He finally fell asleep, but I had trouble settling—so much was spinning around in my head. Eventually, I fell asleep, but I got up to feed Elisha in the early hours and then had trouble returning to sleep. The main thought bothering me was, what if Joe didn't go to the tennis tournament on Sunday? What would I do then? How would the girls and I get out of the house if he was there? Everything depended on him leaving that day. I knew I should leave it with God, and so I prayed that He would work it out. Sleep finally came.

When I woke the next morning, my head ached, but not from a hangover. I had to get up because I could hear the girls in the next room, but Joe was still sound asleep. Waking a drunk is never fun as you never know what they're going to be like, but he couldn't sleep all day—we were moving. I steeled myself and tried to rouse him, praying he'd be in a good mood. Thankfully, when he came to, he was in a reasonable frame of mind, and after a shower and a coffee he was almost human. He said that his mates would be there sometime in the morning to help, so at least he'd remembered.

I felt bad about deceiving him, but there was no choice. I kept reminding myself of Jack's words—I wasn't leaving Joe, he'd already left me. And it was true. Joe had no interest in me or the girls—he said he loved us, but his actions proved otherwise.

So, I went ahead with the plan. Joe's mates arrived with a small truck. They loaded everything into it, drove to the new house, and then unloaded it. Joe, in his usual fashion, told me he wanted to take them down to the pub for a drink to thank them. He wouldn't be long—he'd be back within an hour to help unpack. I didn't say it, but I was thinking "yeah right, whatever." I knew he wouldn't be back in an hour. Who was he kidding? For once, I didn't mind. It was better he wasn't there —I needed to sort out what to take and what to store at Sue and Chris's, and it'd be so much easier without him around.

Katie and Lily were excited to be in the new house. They ran to the backyard and squealed when they saw a cubby house, a swing set and a sandpit. It would have been the perfect house for our little family. So bittersweet. They played happily, leaving me time to think about how to tackle the unpacking and repacking.

Needing to make it look like I was actually putting things

away, I did some of that with the things I planned to leave behind, like plates and small appliances. I'd decided to only put into storage things that were important or expensive to replace, such as gifts the girls had been given, toys too large to take, some of the household items I felt I should keep, and my guitar. I moved all of these items into a separate room and boxed them up as well as I could.

I didn't pack our bags, but I kept the things I'd set aside to take in separate drawers so it wouldn't take long on Sunday morning. I made a list of items to pack at the last minute so I wouldn't forget, and put it at the bottom of one of the drawers —somewhere I didn't think Joe would find it.

I had one more day to go—we moved on the Friday, and so I just had to keep up the charade for another day. As expected, Joe didn't return until much later that afternoon, and then he wasn't good for anything. He started to help but ended up on the couch watching television with Katie and Lily—something he'd done a lot of over the years, especially when he wasn't working.

He dozed, and when he came to, he said he had to go and meet someone, but that he'd try to get back to help before it was too late. Well, he didn't come home until the middle of the night, and since the house was unfamiliar, he fell over things as he staggered in. I was surprised he even found the right house.

Same old routine—he finally fell asleep, and when he got up the next morning, he made a feeble attempt to help unpack, but he wasn't interested. I was relieved when he said he had a practice session with his tennis team in preparation for the tournament the next day. That meant he was intending to go. Relief washed through me.

I asked him how he was getting to the tournament. For a moment I thought he might be planning to take the car, although I doubted he would, as it meant he wouldn't be able to drink. He said that one of his team-mates would collect him at seven a.m. I wondered how he'd be ready that early, but didn't say anything. Casually, I asked what time he thought they might be back, just out of interest. He didn't know but thought maybe about dinner time, but there could be drinks at the end, so maybe even later. So far, so good...

I finished packing and repacking while he was out. I was tired, physically, mentally, and emotionally, so I didn't have much problem stopping and taking a rest, and so when Joe returned later that day, that's how he found me. He said he liked the house, and that he'd try to be at home more often. I bit my lip. He played with the girls for a short while, then said he was going out for an hour or so, but he wouldn't be late. I hoped he'd stay out longer, because I didn't know if I could keep up the charade if he was around, but either way, I had to.

As soon as he left, I telephoned Sue and told her that so far it was going to plan, and I was ready to leave in the morning. We just needed for Joe to actually go to the tennis tournament. The fall back plan was that if he didn't, we assumed he'd probably go out as he normally did, so I'd just have to wait for him to do that. However, because we were booked on the eleven a.m. bus at Cobar, and then flights the following day, there was little margin left for anything to go wrong.

CHAPTER 10

The hour or so turned into six. Joe returned home just before midnight, and for once he wasn't overly drunk. He must have controlled himself because of the tennis tournament, which just proved that if he really wanted to, he could have decided to stop drinking at any time, but we obviously weren't important enough for him to do that. It was all very sad, especially when I thought back to all we'd been through.

I hardly slept that night with everything swirling around in my head. Morning finally came, and as Joe had to be up early to leave for the tournament, I rose too, and so did the girls. We had a quick breakfast together, which was very unusual, and then his mate collected him. I wished him well and as I waved him off, sadness engulfed me. I truly had loved him and had given my life to helping him and trying to make our marriage work. That morning, when he kissed me and looked into my eyes, I saw glimpses of the man I'd fallen in love with. When he was sober, sometimes my heart still fluttered. He was a handsome, intelligent charmer who could have done anything. That was the sorrow of it all. So much potential, wasted.

But it was over. Once I was sure they'd gone, I shoved all of those thoughts to the back of my mind and hurriedly got our bags out and packed them. There wasn't a moment to spare.

Parking the car as close to the house as possible, I felt devious, but I didn't want anyone seeing me putting the bags into the car and asking questions I couldn't give an honest answer to. I got them into the car, but had to tell Katie and Lily we were going on a trip because they looked at me strangely and asked what I was doing. They grew excited but asked if Daddy was coming, too. I told them he wasn't this time, that he'd gone to play tennis with his friends, and we were going to visit some new friends. First, we were going to Sue and Chris's.

Brushing tears from my eyes, my heart pounded as we pulled out of the driveway. I grieved for Joe. He was losing not only his wife but his three little girls. But I was doing the right thing. He'd had so many chances to fix his alcohol and drug problems, but each time he'd drifted back to his old ways. I'd already left four times. This time I couldn't go back.

Hot tears streamed down my cheeks and my throat tightened. For the sake of the girls, I had to pull myself together. How could we make it to the other side of the country if their mother was a blubbering mess? I had to be strong.

I dried my tears and drove through town to Sue and Chris's. Thoughts that Joe might come back for something and catch me in the middle of leaving bombarded my mind. I had no idea what I'd say to him if he did—I prayed it wouldn't come to that.

I made it to Sue and Chris's and parked the car around the back so it wasn't easily visible from the road. Jack was there. He wanted to say goodbye and wish us all the best from everyone at Cornerstone. We didn't stay long—just long enough to say our goodbyes, which were very emotional, and for me to get my instructions in detail.

As we left, Jack handed me another envelope, full of cash. He said to take it, that it was their gift to us, and they didn't need to be repaid. I had no idea how much was in the envelope, but from the weight of it, it felt like a lot. I tried to return it, but he wouldn't hear of it. He said I'd need it—it could be a while before it was safe to claim any benefits, as Joe would surely try to track me through whatever means he could. It would be necessary to keep a low profile for as long as possible.

Sue helped me get the girls into the car, and I pulled myself together enough to drive. Half of me was sorry to be leaving my good friends, especially as I didn't know when I'd see them again, but the other half just wanted to get out of Bourke as quickly as I could. I didn't want anyone to recognise me as I drove through town. Thankfully, the streets were almost empty, and so I prayed it would be okay. When I reached the open road, heading in almost the opposite direction from Joe, I breathed easier, although my heart still pounded.

It was an hour-and-a-half to Cobar, and although the road was sealed, it was narrow and I needed to concentrate. The traffic was light. In fact, I saw only three other vehicles the whole way, so with each minute that passed, confidence grew that we could truly escape to safety.

Not wanting to stop, I'd memorised the instructions of how to find the property where I was to leave the car. Fortunately, I found the place without any problem. A buxom woman with a cheerful demeanour came out from a small, well maintained cottage and greeted us. Although we didn't know each other, it was like we were old friends. Hilda invited us in for some refreshments. We had enough time, so I accepted her offer gratefully. I wasn't looking forward to the twelve-hour bus trip with three little girls.

Hilda told me she'd store my car in one of the sheds on the property, and to let her know, via Jack, when and if I ever wanted to collect it. It could stay there for as long as needed. It wouldn't be in the way, because the shed was no longer used.

After a short break, she drove us to the bus stop in her old truck. She thought it less conspicuous than my car—we didn't want word reaching Joe about what direction we'd taken. We arrived at the bus stop ten minutes before the bus was due. My heart was in my throat as we waited. I felt vulnerable and obvious standing there with the three girls, four suitcases, a pram and a bassinet—we'd be a lot safer once on the bus. I didn't know if Joe had friends in Cobar, but I assumed he did, and so I prayed fervently that no one would recognise us.

The bus finally arrived. With help from the driver, we climbed aboard and settled into our seats. Katie and Lily were excited to start with, but I knew their enthusiasm would wane quickly because there was nothing to see but miles of bare, open space. I'd packed activity books and games, but it was expecting a lot for them to sit still for twelve hours. After a long five hours, we had a two-hour break in Broken Hill. We found a park and Katie and Lily ran off all their energy while I tended to Elisha. All too soon, we boarded the bus again for the next seven-hour stint to Adelaide.

I don't know how we survived that trip, but somehow, we did. It's certainly not one I'd want to repeat with three young children, but we finally arrived in Adelaide late on Sunday night. I'd been told to look out for the middle-aged couple who would take us to their home for the night, and then drive us to the airport the following morning. Don and Maree found us before I found them. I guess we were obvious—a mother on her own with three young children, one of them a three-month-old baby.

It was after midnight when we reached their expansive home in the Adelaide Hills, and I was more than ready for bed. Memories of this couple are clouded, but they opened their home to us and willingly transported us and our luggage to and from the bus depot and the airport without any real idea of who we were. Their willingness to help revealed to me how much respect Jack held amongst his network of friends.

Following a quick breakfast, Don drove us to the airport on his way to work, and we were ready for the next leg of our journey. I was thankful that the flight was only three hours—I don't know how I would have coped with another twelve-hour trip. The girls were well-behaved, but it was a lot to expect of them, especially since they didn't understand what was happening.

Cathy, a friend of the Cornerstone student whose parents'

farm we were going to, met us at Perth airport. About my age, we hit it off immediately. We laughed when we looked at her tiny car and then at the luggage. How would we ever fit it all in, and leave room for the five of us? After a lot of juggling, pushing, and laughing, we managed to squeeze everything in, and we started on the final leg of the journey.

CHAPTER 11

*C*athy and I chatted the whole way, and before we knew it, she was slowing to turn into the farm's driveway. She told me that the farmhouse was about a mile from the road, along a rough dirt track. The realisation that this was our new home hit me, so I sat up and paid attention. Cattle grazed in the front paddock, and in the distance, I glimpsed what I initially thought were sheep, but on second glance, decided they were goats. It didn't take long for the farmhouse to come into sight, and then the car came to a halt and we piled out.

Cathy had visited Bruce and Sharon several times with Laura, their daughter. She made the introductions, and after greeting us, Sharon, a woman of medium height with short, wavy hair tinged with grey, and dressed in faded blue jeans and a smart yellow blouse, invited us to sit under a large shady tree where a feast awaited us. I had to stop Katie and Lily from diving in and helping themselves to the scrumptious looking home-made scones piled high on a plate.

"Oh, come on, let them have as many as they want. They must be hungry after the journey you've all had," Sharon said, as she held out her arms to take Elisha from me.

Right from the beginning, Sharon was taken with the girls, especially Elisha. She had grandchildren of a similar age, and the girls warmed to her immediately. It saddened me that my daughters didn't really know their own grandparents on either side, but it seemed that for a time, Sharon would fill that role. She and Bruce had another daughter, not much older than Katie. Jessica was still at school that afternoon, but Sharon said she was looking forward to meeting the girls when she arrived home.

Bruce was quiet but appeared to be a typical, hard-working farmer. After a few moments, he said he could only take a short break and needed to get back to his tractor. Their teenage son, Ricky, also worked on the farm, and he, too, had to return to work and left with his dad.

That left Sharon, Cathy, myself, and the girls. We all talked at once, but I felt at ease with my new friend and my new "mother". The girls seemed happy to sit, listen and eat, but I could tell they were itching to run around after sitting still for almost two days. Sharon asked if they'd like to see the goats. Their eyes lit up and they nodded eagerly. It was almost milking time, and Ricky was rounding the goat herd up. Jessica arrived home from school just as we were tidying the table. She barely said a word. She obviously took after her father, not her mother, but Katie and Lily were happy to meet someone close to their age, and I had little doubt they'd all become friends.

We all went to watch the goats being rounded up. I had no idea they could be so naughty, but Ricky managed to get them into the pen with the help of his cattle dog, Matilda. The girls were entranced—they'd never seen anything like it. Ricky said we could watch him do the milking if we liked, but he wasn't quite ready to start. Sharon suggested we might want to look at our accommodation and freshen up a little. It sounded like a good idea to me—I was feeling tired after the long trip and could have done with a rest, but was unlikely to get one.

Sharon led us to the building that had been used for the kids' camps. It was only a short distance from the farmhouse but was a completely separate building. We walked up four steps and entered a large room with high, open-beam timber ceilings. Long trestle tables and benches ran along one side, and the remainder of the room was almost bare.

From there we passed through a doorway and entered a small kitchen where a wood stove dominated the room. A smaller table and four chairs sat in the middle. Adjoining the kitchen was another room with three single beds. Sharon apologised that the bathroom was outside. I laughed. After some of the places we'd lived in, this was a mansion, and an outside bathroom was nothing. Although not as cozy as a house, I was thankful to have somewhere safe to stay. I knew we'd be comfortable, but cooking on a wood stove concerned me a little. When I voiced my concerns, Sharon promised to show me how to use it and told me not to worry.

Sharon and Cathy brought our bags in as I tended to Elisha.

Sharon had already made the beds and had also provided some basic food items in the kitchen. It didn't take long to unpack, so we soon returned outside to watch Ricky milk the goats. He was halfway through when we arrived at the milking shed, and he asked Katie and Lily if they'd like to have a try. They giggled and clung to me. They'd never seen a cow or a goat milked before, let alone touch a goat's teat. I pushed them forward and encouraged them to have a go, which they did, without much success. Ricky said they could try again another day if they wanted.

It was starting to get late, and Cathy said she needed to get going since she had to drive back to Perth. I was sad to see her leave, but she promised to visit when she could, and said we'd always be welcome at her place if we were able to get to Perth for a few days.

Sharon invited us to eat dinner with them that night. Despite their welcome, I felt I was intruding on their close-knit family, but I was thankful for their hospitality and willingness to open their home to us.

Knowing we were tired after our long trip, once dinner was finished, Sharon suggested we might like to head off for an early night. I was grateful for her understanding and awareness, and after thanking them all for their hospitality, we returned to our "house".

As I bathed the girls in the outside bathroom, I knew that this was the start of my new life as a solo parent. I'd finally done it. I'd left Joe, and I wasn't returning. I wondered what he'd done when he came home after the tennis tournament to find us gone. I planned to call Sue the next morning to let her know we'd arrived safely and to find out what had happened, so until then, I felt safe and secure knowing that there was no way he could have found us in that short a time.

After I settled the girls into their beds, I made a pot of tea and sat at the kitchen table. Without a television or radio, all I could hear were the outside farm noises and the heavy breathing of the girls as they slept. I struggled to keep my eyes open, and although I'd planned to read, I soon joined them.

Not being used to sleeping in the same room with them, and despite my exhaustion, sleep eluded me. I must have fallen asleep eventually, because before I knew it, sunlight was streaming in through the flimsy curtains and the girls were jumping on my bed. They pleaded with me to let them see the goats being milked again.

Managing to calm them, I gave them a quick breakfast before we ventured outside. It was such a beautiful place in the early morning. Birds flying overhead twittered to each other, cattle bellowed in the distance, goats bleated, and chooks clucked. The girls ran around not knowing which way to go first.

Sharon waved to us from outside her house and joined me, holding her arms out to Elisha as she approached. At three months, Elisha was starting to be aware of her surroundings, and she gurgled happily when Sharon took her and spoke to her animatedly. "She's a gorgeous baby, Julie. In fact, all three of your girls are gorgeous."

I was about to tell her they got their looks from their father, but I hesitated. I wasn't ready to talk with her about Joe just yet. It was too fresh and raw, and I didn't want to end in tears, so I just smiled and thanked her.

As we stood watching Katie and Lily explore the area in

front of the building, I asked Sharon about the farm. She told me that they derived most of their income from potatoes and onions. They kept the animals mainly for their own use, although they did sell some of the goats' milk to a shop in town. They also sold some cattle each year when possible. They'd been farmers all their lives but had only been on this particular farm for ten years.

"We love it here. The ocean's less than a mile away. Not that we manage to get there often." She let out a chuckle. "And the nearest town isn't far. And our eldest daughter and her husband live nearby. It's hard work, but we love it."

I asked if I could use her phone to call Sue when it was convenient. She said that was fine, and that led to a discussion about how we'd ended up in this situation.

Despite my earlier intention not to do so, over coffee, I told her about Joe and his drinking problems, and all the things we'd tried over the years, and that although I'd left several times before, each time he either found me or I'd given in and contacted him, but nothing ever changed. The only solution was to get so far away that he wouldn't come after me, and I wouldn't be tempted to contact him. Since Joe could be volatile and unpredictable, especially when drunk, my main concern was for the girls. I didn't want them growing up in that kind of environment.

"I'm so sorry to hear all that. You should be safe here, and the girls will have a ball. And if ever you need a break, I'd love to mind them."

I felt so very blessed and grateful for this kind and under-standing woman, and for the opportunity to live in such a wonderful place. It was more than I could ever have hoped for or deserved.

When I called Sue a short while later, my voice faltered. It seemed such a long time since I'd left her place and started the long journey, but only two days had passed. And now here I was, on the other side of the country, thousands of miles from Joe.

Sue told me that when he arrived home after the tennis tournament and found us gone, he immediately went to their place, but they'd been prepared for him. Chris told him that yes, they knew we'd gone, but no, they wouldn't tell him where we were, now or ever, and that if he caused any trouble, they'd call the police. Joe abused them verbally, but when they started to phone the police, he calmed down and left.

He returned the following day, but Sue told him exactly the same thing. I felt terrible that I'd placed her and the kids in danger. Joe could easily have hurt them, but something had stopped him. She said he looked despondent, but he'd told her before he left that he'd get all of his mates tracking us down and he wouldn't stop until he found us. She promised to let me know if he left Bourke, and she'd try to find out if he had any idea about where we might have gone. In the meantime, I wasn't to worry, as it seemed he had no clue whatsoever. She promised to call every few days with an update.

I felt so relieved. At least I knew Joe was still in Bourke, and that even if he left and knew where I was, it would take him at least two days to get here, so for the time being, I felt safe.

After I ended the call, Sharon said that she and Bruce would like to have a chat with me about what I would do while I lived on the farm. She suggested we get together after lunch as Bruce usually took an hour off at that time. I said that was fine with me—I didn't have any other plans.

I wondered what they might suggest. Housework? Gardening? I was gob-smacked when they suggested I take over the goats. Why did they think I could possibly do that? I'd never seen a goat milked before we arrived, let alone know how to do it.

Bruce said it would be the most helpful job I could do because it was taking up too much of Ricky's time. He needed his son to help more with the potatoes and onions, and milking the goats would not only free up Ricky's time but would help pay my way. I hesitantly agreed after telling him I had no idea how to do it and had never been around goats in my life.

"That's okay. Ricky can show you the ropes and won't leave you on your own until you feel comfortable."

I felt only slightly better.

I wondered what I'd do with the girls, especially Elisha, while I milked them. Western Australian has different starting ages for school, and although Katie had started school in Bourke, she wasn't old enough to attend school in WA until the following year, so all three girls would be at home. Bruce suggested I take Elisha with me in her pram, but that Lily and Katie would be okay to play around the farmhouse as long as they stayed inside the fences. He said I should start that afternoon. It seemed I didn't have a choice.

He then asked how I would look after myself. His bluntness surprised me, but I'd already gathered that their finances were tight. I didn't want to be a burden, and at that moment I was very grateful for the money Jack had given me. I told Bruce and Sharon about it and said it should last a few months if I was careful. They seemed relieved, and Bruce visibly relaxed. He told me I could have fresh goats' milk every day and as many eggs, potatoes, and onions as we could use. If I wanted to help tend the vegetable garden, I could also take some of the produce. I thanked them, ever so grateful for their kindness.

Sharon planned a trip to town the next day. She suggested I go with her to get some groceries and she would also show me around at the same time. And just like that, it was settled. I would milk the goats, morning and afternoon, and if needed, I could go into town with Sharon once a week. Other than that, I could work in the veggie garden, and then do whatever other odd jobs I could find.

Bruce suggested that Katie could help Jessica look after the chooks. Jessica, one year older than Katie, had lived on the farm all her life. She was used to doing jobs around the farm before and after school. When I told Katie about her "job", she was thrilled and couldn't wait until Jessica got home to start.

After our chat, Bruce returned to work and I prepared for my next challenge—learning how to milk goats. Sharon offered to mind the girls for the first few days while I learned. I was grateful for this, as I knew I'd need to focus. Ricky told me that the goats could be quite naughty, and I had to learn the tricks of the trade to get them to do what I wanted them to do. Just like teaching…or so I thought.

CHAPTER 12

There were twenty-four nanny goats, whom I'd met, and one billy goat I had yet to meet, but from what Ricky told me about his disgusting habits, like peeing on his face to make himself attractive to the nannies, I had no great desire to ever come face to face with him. Thankfully, my job was with the nannies, and they all had names. I doubted I'd ever learn them all, but Ricky assured me they all had individual personalities and looks, just like kids, and that I'd gradually sort out who was who.

My first job was to round them up. They stayed mainly in the paddock closest to the farmhouse, and like cows, usually knew when it was milking time. Some of them were cantankerous and wouldn't follow the others into the pen. When this happened, Ricky used Matilda, his cattle dog, to whip them into line. However, I wouldn't be able to do this, as Matilda always stayed with him. The best thing for me to use was a long switch branch from one of the Geraldton Wax trees.

Ricky assured me the branches didn't hurt the goats, but a quick flick on their rumps got them moving. I wondered how I'd ever manage to get them all into the pen at the same time, let alone milk them.

Once he herded them in the pen, he showed me how to prepare the milk pails, how to call the goats in one by one, and then how to sit and hold their teats. Fortunately, each goat only had two teats, not four, like a cow, so it was quicker than milking a cow, not that I'd ever done that, either. He then showed me how to start squeezing, and what rhythm to use, and then how to strip the teat after most of the milk had been released so they wouldn't get mastitis.

It was all so foreign, but after a few attempts I started to get the hang of it. Soon, my hands ached. Fortunately, I didn't have to milk all twenty-four to start with, which I was very thankful for, however, still having to milk fifteen was overwhelming. The other nannies would need milking once they had their kids over the next few weeks.

Ricky emphasised how important it was to empty the teats, but he told me to be careful not to squeeze too high as I could injure them and they could get infected. My mind whirled.

Once finished, I had to clean and hose down the area and sterilize the equipment. He'd show me how to do all of that another day. I breathed a sigh of relief. We then placed the milk pails into the fridge, ready for Sharon to sort out. By the time we'd finished, I was exhausted, but also amazed I could actually do this. Never in my wildest dreams had I ever expected to be milking a herd of goats by hand!

While I'd been occupied with the goats, Jessica had taken Katie to clean out the chook pen, a job Katie thought was fun to start with. As the months wore on, her opinion changed and she became less eager.

And so started our daily routine. I grew more confident with the goats and rounded them up fairly quickly, although some days they were naughtier than others, and it took longer than it should to get them all into the pen. My hands became stronger and I grew more skilled with the milking. I also learned all the nannies' names and knew which ones I needed to be wary of, and which ones were always friendly. Elisha was happy to sit in her pram and watch me work, as long as she had drink and food to keep her going. Katie and Lily looked forward to Jessica coming home each day so they could play together once they'd completed their jobs.

Sue kept her word and called every few days to update me on Joe's activities. For the first couple of weeks, he was continually drunk but hadn't caused too much trouble. He did, however, lose his job. Then one day, he disappeared. Someone said they thought he'd caught a lift with one of his mates to Sydney, but they weren't sure. He'd left the house in a mess, but Sue said that she and Chris cleaned it and that her father was sorting it out with the owners, and for me not to worry. I was so grateful, but I felt terrible they had to do this.

Not knowing Joe's whereabouts concerned me. They didn't think he knew where we were and thought we'd be fine, but that didn't stop the panic attacks in the middle of the night when everything was quiet, and I imagined I could hear noises like someone trying to break in.

I'd moved out of the bedroom I shared with the girls and into the big open dining hall several weeks earlier as I found it difficult to sleep in the same room as them. But when I'd heard that Joe had left Bourke, I felt vulnerable out there on my own, so I moved back in with the girls. I was being silly, but I couldn't stop the dread that came over me at night. I'd heard about alcoholic husbands attacking their wives and kids, and I knew what Joe was capable of. Even though I prayed for protection, I still felt concerned. I didn't know how he'd track us down, but I knew that if he really put his mind to it, he probably could.

I shared with Bruce and Sharon my concerns over the possibility of Joe finding us, and what he might do if he did. They seemed to understand but assured me that if anyone tried to approach the farmhouse during the night, the dogs would hear and make a fuss. They tried to assure me it would be okay, and they'd be there if anything happened.

Weeks passed, and we continued with our routine. Each morning I rose early to round up and milk the goats. When the girls woke, Katie ran down to the shed to let me know they were up so I could get Elisha. Most mornings, I finished before they woke. We then ate breakfast, and after a short devotion, walked either to the beach or explored the surrounding bushland before returning to do our chores.

After lunch, we had an afternoon rest, and then the girls went to Sharon while I rounded up the goats again for the afternoon milking session. The girls then bathed, and following dinner, we played games and read books before saying our evening prayers. I was so enjoying spending quality time with my precious daughters.

Once they were in bed, I settled in for an evening with a good book. There was no television, but I'd bought a radio cassette player, so at least I could listen to music. One day a week, we went into town with Sharon to do our shopping.

Although we had this regular routine, Joe was constantly on my mind. I found myself searching for him in the distance, thinking he might be out there somewhere. I had this dreadful feeling he'd find me. One day I gave in and called his sister, Lisa. I was taking a risk, but not knowing his whereabouts was torture.

I called from a pay phone so it would be harder to track where I'd called from—not that I expected she'd tell him, but it was possible he could answer. He wasn't there, and she didn't know where he was. She said he'd called a few weeks earlier and told her he was in Sydney somewhere, but he was drunk and she couldn't make sense out of anything he said. I told her I wasn't going back this time, but I was concerned he'd find me, so it was better she didn't know where I was. That way, if he asked her, she could honestly say she didn't know. Fortunately for me, his sisters were on "my side". They knew what Joe had put me through all those years, and I think they felt a degree of guilt, since it was through them we'd met.

I also called my parents. I knew they'd be worried about us, but once again, I didn't tell them where we were so that they, too, could honestly say they didn't know if Joe turned up on their doorstep. It felt strange that almost no one, including my family, knew my whereabouts. Just a handful of people in Bourke knew, and they weren't saying a word.

My parents were relieved that I'd finally made the decision to leave Joe for good, but were understandably concerned about me and the girls. But there was little they could do while I was in hiding.

Life went on. One day, Bruce and Sharon asked if I'd like to borrow their second car one day a week so I could go into town on my own. I'd started to feel hemmed in, so I jumped at this offer. The idea of going out on my own with the girls filled me with excitement. I was given strict guidelines, but that was okay. Even if I had the car for half a day a week, it was better than nothing.

The first time I ventured into town on my own, I felt a strange sense of freedom. I was starting to get an idea of what life could be like without the constant fear of what Joe was doing hanging over me like a cloud. The worst thing about having an alcoholic husband was never knowing when he'd come home, and what he'd do when he did. I'd lived in constant dread and fear. Now, I had hope that all that was over for good. I knew I wouldn't go back. I couldn't, even if I wanted to—not after all the money and effort that had gone into helping me escape. My main concern was what would happen if Joe tracked me down.

I attended the local church with Sharon and Bruce, and although it was small, I made some friends who invited me to their playgroup. I started taking the girls, and we often stayed for lunch at one of the ladies' homes. A strong friendship developed with one of the women. Anna was several years older than me, but she had young children much the same age, and we got on well. Although I couldn't spend much time with her, I appreciated her friendship, as I was starting to feel lonely and isolated. I began teaching Sunday School, and Anna found me a spare guitar and I helped lead the morning worship service with her.

My life was slowly rebuilding. I had plenty of spare time to deal with the underlying issues that had resulted in me being where I was. Anna was very helpful and encouraged me to think deeply about things, such as working out what needed changing in myself so I wouldn't be as vulnerable in the future. I'd worked through some of this in Bourke, but now that I'd actually left Joe, there were other things to consider. I knew I had to forgive him for all he'd done to me, and I had to forgive Greg and his mother. I also had to forgive my dad for not being the loving father I wanted him to be. Not only did I need to forgive them, I had to let go. That was almost harder than forgiving.

Living in such a peaceful and beautiful place, and having plenty of time to enjoy it, gave me the opportunity to turn my life around. Having the support and friendship of Sharon, Bruce and Anna, as well as others, gave me the ability to grow as a person, and to know that I could make a life for myself and the girls on my own. I was an intelligent young woman who'd made some stupid mistakes and had paid the price. I'd been given the opportunity to get out of the gutter I'd been living in with Joe for so many years, and I was grasping it with open arms.

Months passed, and the money Jack had given me was almost gone. I knew I'd need to register for the Supporting Parents' Benefit before long. That concerned me, as it meant coming out of hiding since my address would then be updated on the central Social Security register. The eldest of Joe's three sisters worked for Social Security, and although I doubted Rebekah could access my details, I didn't think she'd give them to Joe, even if she could. Still, that thought lingered in the back of my mind. But I didn't have a choice. I needed money to live and to support the girls.

Not long after, I told my parents where we were—they were shocked we were so far away. They were on the east coast, I was on the west. My dad was coming to the west with his job for a few days and said he'd stay a little longer and visit. I wasn't sure how I'd handle him seeing me in this situation. I'd failed. He and my mother had held such high hopes for me when I left school and went to University. I was the first one on both sides of the family, apart from one of my mother's cousins, to do that, and they were proud. And then I messed up. Anna said I needed to forgive myself too... I guess I did.

When my dad arrived a few weeks later, I grew quite emotional. Because we'd never been a family that showed much emotion, he didn't know how to handle my tears, but he seemed pleased to see that we were okay. I finally managed to pull myself together and showed him around the farm. Although the girls didn't know him well, they were happy to see him and were eager to show him the chook pen and the goats.

Being a practical person, he asked if I needed anything. I jokingly said yes—a car. In my younger days, I'd driven myself everywhere. I'd passed my driving test on my seventeenth birthday, and loved the freedom of being able to drive anywhere I wanted. Before I met Joe, I'd driven between Sydney and Brisbane, and then Brisbane and Gladstone, so often I could have driven the road blindfolded. Not having my own car was a constant source of frustration to me, but I didn't expect him to help me get one. I was only joking.

But Dad being Dad told me to leave it with him. He was a

motor mechanic by trade, and so cars were right up his alley. Within two days, he'd found a very reasonably priced old Ford Falcon in good condition—he'd checked it over thoroughly, and said we could collect it that day. I was so excited I could hardly contain myself.

He couldn't stay long as he had work commitments, but his visit gave me hope that a new life lay ahead of me. He asked if I had any idea how long I would stay on the farm. At that stage, I didn't know. I told him I'd stay until I felt confident that Joe wouldn't track us down and I felt safe returning to the east coast. I had no idea how long that would take, but I thought it would be at least another six months, at which time I'd also be able to apply for a divorce. He then asked if I'd thought about where I'd go when we left.

"You'd be welcome to stay with me and Mum for a while if need be," he said. I hadn't expected that, and it brought tears to my eyes. I thanked him and said I'd probably accept the offer.

Before he left, he told me that Mum and my brother, Graham, were thinking of visiting early the following year. Tears once again built behind my eyes, but although the news overwhelmed me, I didn't cry.

With Christmas approaching, I had a longing to spend it with my family, but it was too soon to go home. Over the years, Joe and I had had very few 'good' Christmases—he usually ended up drunk or stoned, causing tension with what-ever family we were with. I determined that the girls and I would have a good Christmas, regardless. Bruce and Sharon invited us to join them for Christmas lunch. I felt we were intruding on their family, but Sharon was adamant we should join them, so we did.

The girls and I had our own little Christmas tree which they helped to decorate, and Christmas morning was full of fun and anticipation as they opened their presents. I vowed that this was the start of a completely new life. One that wasn't controlled by an alcoholic husband, but one filled with happiness, free from fear.

As it hadn't been long since my dad's visit, and with my mother and brother's visit looming, I began to think seriously about what I would do, and when. I needed to stay away for at least a year so I could file for divorce. Reluctant to venture anywhere near where Joe might be, I considered my dad's offer. Because I'd seen so little of my parents all the time Joe and I had been together, and when we did see them, he'd usually behaved badly, and because they'd seen very little of their grandchildren, I decided it was the right thing to do.

I just had to be patient, which was becoming increasingly difficult. I started feeling that I was outstaying my welcome at the farm. Not that it was ever said directly—I just got that feeling. When I'd first arrived, both Bruce and Sharon had said I was welcome to stay as long as needed, and no specific length of time had been mentioned, but maybe they hadn't imagined I'd be there for more than a few months.

I counted down the days until my mother and brother's arrival. Once again, I felt overwhelmed when I saw them. I think they were relieved to see I was fit and healthy, and that the girls were thriving in their new environment. They were staying for five days, so we decided to take a trip in my big old car and have a short holiday together.

It was a strange time, as I hadn't seen Graham since his marriage had failed, and he was still trying to sort himself out.

Then here was me with the three girls, trying to work out what we were going to do. And my poor mum, she must have wondered where she'd gone wrong with us both. We had a lovely few days together touring the south-west corner of Western Australia, but before I knew it, I was back on my own, starting the countdown.

I placed a calendar on the wall and crossed off each day before I got into bed at night...it seemed like such a long time before I could go 'home'. I enjoyed living on the farm, but it was only temporary, and I felt like I was biding my time, almost as if I was in exile. I kept telling myself it was necessary —I hadn't been away from Joe long enough, and I didn't want to risk going back to the east coast too early.

I spent whatever time I could with Anna, but she lived a busy life, so I had to occupy myself with chores around the place, walking, reading and writing. I had plenty of time to read and write since the girls went to bed early, and so I had night after night to myself.

Bruce took it upon himself to be my counsellor, and he often cornered me when I walked back from the goats or from the veggie garden. He didn't agree with me wanting to divorce Joe. He'd thought I was just taking a break, and that I'd return after sorting through some issues. I truly don't know where he'd gotten that idea from. I tried to explain why I couldn't return, but he told me I was going against God if I went through with it. He was also annoyed now that I had my own car that I could go out whenever I wanted. He and Sharon couldn't do that because they had so many chores to do. Not that I went out often. I went into town twice a week, and I played netball with Anna's team on a Saturday afternoon, so I drove myself there, as well as playgroup and Bible study. But it was enough to cause friction. I promised to be more helpful and considerate, but underneath I wondered how much longer I could put up with Bruce's constant attack on my character, which is what I perceived it to be.

The days rolled by, and slowly my calendar filled with crosses. It was quite sad, now I think about it, but although I was very thankful for the opportunity to make that final break from Joe, I was growing increasingly impatient to start my new life. Impatience had always been one of my negative qualities and was one of the causes of my getting into this situation in the first place. I was certainly aware of that and asked God to teach me patience and to enjoy each day as it came.

The girls were my life, and I loved them so much. I felt terrible about the start in life I'd given them. It certainly wasn't the ideal situation in which to raise children, but they seemed resilient and showed no obvious signs of emotional trauma. Katie had asked a few times where Daddy was, and I'd told her the truth—that Daddy hadn't been the daddy he should have been, and that we needed to be happy on our own, without him. She was old enough to know that things hadn't been good when he was around, and she didn't seem to have a problem with him not being with us. I certainly made every effort to provide a stable environment for them—I didn't want them growing up with issues that could haunt them for the rest of their lives. I prayed constantly that God would protect them from the trauma of their past.

Another issue caught up with me during this time. As I'd been the one with the stable income in the early days of our marriage, the loans we'd taken out for the caravan and cars were in my name. The insurance company hadn't paid out on any of Joe's accidents since he'd been driving under the influence. I don't know how we managed to continue getting loans, but somehow, we did, and although my parents had helped out a few times when we'd gotten behind on payments, I came to the conclusion that there was no way I could repay the debt now owing. As I'd been in hiding and hadn't changed my address or contact details with any of the institutions, I'd been able to ignore the situation, but slowly, they were finding me, and I couldn't hide any longer.

I wasn't in a situation where I could return to work. Elisha was just over twelve-months old, and because I was planning on returning 'home' in the near future, it wasn't right to seek employment at that point in time. I made the gut-wrenching decision to declare myself bankrupt. I had nothing other than my old Ford Falcon, which was only worth two-hundred dollars, so there was nothing I could sell to repay any of the money I owed. I felt bad it had come to this. I hadn't been brought up to shirk my responsibilities, but there was no way I could repay the outstanding debt. In reality, the debts were Joe's responsibility. He was the one who'd written off the cars and hadn't kept a steady job, but since the loans were in my name, it *was* my problem.

So, I became bankrupt. Being an optimist, I believed that although this was a bad situation to be in, it wouldn't last forever. It was a means to an end, so I didn't allow myself to become depressed. I had nothing, anyway, so being bankrupt had no real impact on my life, apart from taking away the pressure of trying to repay loans I couldn't afford. It wiped my slate clean, although I knew I'd carry the stigma for the next seven years.

Finally, the twelve months were up and I was ready to file for divorce. Bruce was adamant he wouldn't allow me to do that while I lived with them. He felt so strongly about it, and although it had nothing to do with him, I didn't think I should go against his wishes since he and Sharon had been so generous in sharing their home with us.

It wasn't a pleasant time and it caused friction. However, I knew beyond a shadow of a doubt it was the right thing for me to do. There was no way I was going back to Joe. I had a clear conscience. He'd had every opportunity to sort himself out, but he chose not to, and instead, he'd chosen a life that didn't include his wife and children. The girls' wellbeing was my main concern, and although I knew children should have a father in their lives, I also knew that having no father was better than having one who was an irresponsible, volatile drunk.

Even though I hadn't wanted to return home until the divorce was final, given the situation, I had to rethink that choice. It seemed that Joe had disappeared. Not even his sisters or parents had heard from him for months. It was unnerving not knowing where he was, however, it did suggest to me that he'd given up trying to find me.

I decided I'd have to go back home and then file for divorce, and pray that Joe didn't turn up and cause trouble in the meantime. With help from my dad, we started working out how the children and I would return to the east coast. As it was too far to drive, he organised for the car to be trucked back with most of our belongings in it, which solved that problem, and it was agreed that the girls and I would fly.

I'd kept in touch with Cathy on and off over the previous twelve months and had been to her place once or twice. When she heard we needed to get to the airport, she offered to drive down and collect us. It seemed like déjà vu, only in reverse!

In the days leading up to our departure, I reflected on all that had happened over the past year or so. It still amazed me that Sue and Jack and the others in Bourke had been so very helpful and supportive. Without them, I don't know that I could have made the break, or if I'd tried on my own, whether it would have been successful. I owed them so much. All the people who helped me out on my "great escape"—people I'd probably never see again, but who'd been prepared to do their bit to help us on our way. Sharon and Bruce, who'd opened up their home to us so willingly, and who, despite our differences of opinion, had provided us with a safe haven for over twelve months.

The personal and spiritual development opportunities I'd experienced were priceless. There had been plenty of time to address those issues in my life that had contributed to my being in that position, and I felt more stable and content than I'd ever been before. I'd spent a huge amount of time reading, especially at night time, and I'd also spent much time journaling, writing down my thoughts and feelings, and giving them to God. I felt more secure in my relationship with Him, and I knew He had a plan for my life, even though I'd messed some of it up. I was so grateful He was in the business of offering second, third, and even fourth, chances.

I'd learned new skills, not least of which was how to milk a goat—twenty-four of them, no less. Bruce and Sharon had finally upgraded to an electric milking system a few months earlier, and it made my job a whole lot easier, but I still had to round up the goats, "hook them up", and then clean them. The girls had witnessed the birth of baby kids and had the opportunity to bottle-feed some of them. Katie had spent a lot of time with the chooks and knew what it was like to have a daily job that had to be done, whether she liked it or not. We'd spent a lot of time in the outdoors, walking either in the paddocks or along the beach. We'd played games together, read together, and I eventually relaxed in the freedom of not worrying about when and if Joe would turn up.

It had been a very special time, although I'd had my battles with impatience, but it had been necessary, not only to get away from Joe, but for me to have the opportunity to rebuild my own life without the pressures and distractions of living and working in the city surrounded by people. I'd needed the time out to regroup and refresh before moving on.

CHAPTER 13

$\mathcal{M}$oving day came. Cathy arrived, and we all shared morning tea together, reminiscent of the day she'd brought us down in her tiny car more than a year ago. This time, she'd come prepared with a larger car. There were tears all around as we eventually said our goodbyes. Sharon had developed a strong bond with the girls and was sad to see them leave. I thanked her and Bruce profusely for allowing us to stay, and promised I'd write to let them know how we were doing.

As we drove to the front gate for the last time, my thoughts turned to the future. What would it hold? What would my life look like this time next year? One thing I knew—I needed to trust God to lead and guide me. I needed to make good decisions and not repeat the bad decisions of my past. Anticipation and hope for the future filled me. I couldn't wait to start my new life.

The five-hour flight to Brisbane brought me back to reality.

Elisha, now an active toddler, didn't sit still for more than a few moments at a time. I tried reading to her, but I spent most of the time walking up and down the aisle, holding her. Fortunately, Katie and Lily were well behaved and occupied themselves with the activity packs that the air-hostesses gave them.

My parents were at the airport to meet us, and there were hugs and kisses all around. They were happy to see us and had prepared the house for the arrival of three very active little girls as best they could. I hadn't seen the new house they'd moved into while I was in Bourke, but it was a very nice, modern, two-storey home.

We had three bedrooms on the upstairs level. Katie and Lily shared one, and Elisha and I had separate rooms. The new house, although lovely, felt clinical after the basic accommodation we'd lived in for the past few years—the caravans at Cornerstone, Bourke, then the kids' camp at Sharon and Bruce's. The girls weren't used to being confined to a small room after having the large open area in the camp, and it was a struggle to keep them from running around inside the house. Not that they were naughty, but they'd been so used to living on the farm with wide open spaces, that living in a tidy, orderly house with a small backyard quickly proved a challenge.

It was strange living in the same house as my parents after so many years living away. I'm sure they found it a challenge as well, as their routine was disturbed. Not that they complained, and they said they were enjoying getting to know their grand-daughters, but it wasn't as relaxing as I thought it would be.

Not long after I arrived in Brisbane, I filed my divorce papers. I thought there might be a problem since I didn't have an address for Joe and the papers were meant to be served on him. This caused me some concern as I could imagine what his reaction would be. However, I was told that if I didn't know his whereabouts, and as long as I'd made every effort to locate him, I simply needed to lodge a declaration to that effect and all would be well.

A piece of paper confirming we were no longer married wouldn't stop Joe from doing anything stupid if he got it into his mind to do so, but not having to serve divorce papers on him made me feel safer. I waited patiently for the final decree to come through, which it did, two months later.

I finally felt free, although there was always that little nagging thought at the back of my mind...what would happen when and if he ever came after me? It wouldn't be me he'd be wanting—it would be the girls, so I was constantly vigilant. Whenever they were out of my sight, I was anxious and didn't relax until they were with me again. Although I was probably being overly cautious, I'd never forgive myself if something happened to them. It wouldn't be that difficult for him to find us. I'd taken a risk returning, but there'd been little option other than staying in hiding for the rest of my life. So, I lived each day knowing that while on paper we were divorced, in reality, danger still lurked.

As the months passed, I knew I couldn't stay with my parents for much longer. Not that they complained, but I was constantly reminding the girls to be careful of the walls, not to run inside, and to be careful of this and that. We needed more space, not only physically—I needed to take more control of my life. I needed my own house, but that was out of the question, since I still wasn't working with the girls so young and child care costs so high. I considered applying for public housing, but quickly discovered it would be years before I'd make it to the top of the list. Having lost touch with my university and church friends, I had no one to share with.

As I pondered and prayed over what to do, my brother bought a house and said we could live with him—a real and unexpected answer to prayer.

We moved in several weeks later. We got on well, and as it was an older house, I didn't have to constantly watch what the girls were doing. Not that I allowed them to run around wild. It just didn't matter if they happened to mark the walls, or if they decided to have a rough and tumble game in the lounge room. The backyard, although small, was still large enough for them to run around in, so all in all, it was a great move.

As Graham's house wasn't in the same area as my parents', Katie had to change schools, *again*. This was her fourth in less than two years. I felt terrible and prayed that this would be the last change of schools for a long, long time. I didn't want her education to suffer as a result of all the changes.

We quickly settled into a stable routine. Graham had a steady job, so he went to work each morning, I took Katie to school, and then I came back with Lily and Elisha to do the housework, shopping, and all the normal routine jobs of a stay-at-home mum. I cooked dinner most nights, but I didn't mind. Living a normal life was enjoyable, even if it was with my brother.

Graham was dating a girl he'd met at church, and his and Marie's relationship soon became serious. Marie had a daughter from a previous marriage who was much the same age as Katie and Lily, so whenever they visited, the girls enjoyed playing together. Marie and I became close, but I did start to wonder what I'd do if she and Graham decided to marry. The house wasn't big enough for all of us.

I hadn't been thinking about finding another partner for myself. No one would look at a bankrupt woman with three young children. Besides, I wasn't ready. Having my heart broken by Greg and my spirit almost destroyed by Joe, I was in no hurry to enter another relationship. I'd learned that I didn't need a man in my life to feel loved. God loved me, and that was enough. If only I'd understood the truth of that years earlier.

But it seemed God had other plans.

I'd started going to a church near Graham's house. As well as convenient, one of the ministers happened to be the brother of one of my good friends from Gladstone. I'd met Ron and his wife, Lenore, a few times when they visited his sister, and I thought it could be helpful going to a church where at least one person knew a little of my background in case I needed help at some stage, although I sincerely hoped and prayed I'd never need it.

I joined the church's playgroup and a women's Bible study group, and slowly made new friends. After a short while, Lenore invited me to a new group starting in their home. I was interested, but it was in the evenings. After discussing my dilemma with Graham, he offered to mind the girls so I could go.

It was strange going out without the girls, and as I climbed out of my car and approached Ron and Lenore's home for the first meeting, I took a calming breath. Lenore welcomed me with a kiss and a hug at the door. We'd spent some time together since I'd started going to the church, and I'd shared with her some of what I'd been through. Other than Graham and Marie, she was my closest friend at the time.

About a dozen people, mostly couples, were already seated in their lounge room. They all looked up and smiled as I entered. I quickly chose a seat beside a lady I'd met at playgroup.

After Ron welcomed everyone and opened in prayer, he asked us all to introduce ourselves. I can't remember exactly what I said, but it must have been something fairly inane, like "Hi, my name's Julie. I'm recently divorced, and I've just moved back to Brisbane with my three little girls. I'm a school teacher, but I haven't worked for quite a while." There was no way I could have talked about all I'd been through in a minute or so, nor did I want to.

I listened with interest to what everyone said. We each had different stories, but one man's, in particular, grabbed my attention. Maybe it was his deep voice, or maybe it was that he'd recently arrived in Brisbane after spending several years in the Solomon Islands. Robert's two sons had come with him and were watching television in another room. He didn't say what he did, but I assumed he was a missionary. He also didn't mention a wife, although I assumed he had one.

After the introductions, Bill led a study and prayer time before supper. Robert offered his apologies to the group and left early because the boys had school the next day. I thought nothing more of him.

Sunday came, and the girls and I went to church as usual. Noticing Robert sitting on the other side of the chapel with his teenage boys, I began wondering about his wife. It was unusual seeing a man alone with two sons. Maybe she was still in the Solomon's and would join them soon.

At the end of the service, I collected the girls from Sunday school, but as I walked out with them, I bumped into Robert. "Oh, hello."

"Hello. Julie, isn't it?"

I was surprised he remembered my name. We chatted briefly, but the girls were tugging on my arm, so I apologized and said I had to go.

We saw each other again at the midweek meeting, and this time, since the boys hadn't come, Robert stayed for supper and we chatted again, this time longer. We seemed drawn to each other. Maybe it was because everyone else had a partner, I'm not sure, but I found myself glancing at his left hand, which was bare. That didn't mean anything, and besides, we were just chatting. But the longer we spoke, the more he intrigued me.

He'd lived in the Solomon's for three years, heading up the Telecommunications Training Centre—he wasn't a missionary, after all. And then he told me what I needed to know…his marriage had broken down during those three years, and his wife had moved away with a friend but hadn't taken the boys. Robert had moved to Australia so they could go to school here. I thought it strange that a mother would leave her children, but I didn't comment. He was doing his best to make a new life in Brisbane for himself and the boys, but I sensed deep hurt in his soft, hazel eyes.

I shared a little of my own story, and then it was time to leave. We bid each other good night, but as our gazes met, the sincerity in Robert's eyes made my pulse skitter, taking me by surprise. I tried to hide my reaction, but I snatched a glance at him as he got into his car.

Thoughts of him stayed with me that night as I tried to sleep. I wasn't ready to be any more than friends with him, but after all I'd been through with Joe, it was nice talking with a 'normal' man—and a handsome one at that.

I found myself eagerly awaiting Sunday. Finally, it came, and I was glad to see Robert and the boys sitting in the same section of the chapel as the previous week. At the end of the service, we bumped into each other again, either accidentally or on purpose, I'm not sure which, but we laughed. Robert asked if I'd like coffee. I said I would, and I sent Katie and Lily to the playground. Elisha wanted to follow her sisters, but at eighteen months, she was too little to go without me, so I jiggled her on my hip and gave her a biscuit and hoped she'd stay still.

Robert's boys stood with a group of teens in the courtyard and didn't seem in a hurry to leave.

"How was your week?" he casually asked.

I shrugged and said it was fairly normal…just the usual. "How about yours?"

He told me that while he was applying for jobs in his chosen field of electronics, he was working as an insurance salesman. He didn't particularly like the job, but the bills had to be paid. So different from Joe who didn't know or care what a bill was.

After a while, Robert cleared his throat, and in his deep voice, invited me to his work's Christmas party.

I blinked, thinking I'd misheard.

"It's...it's in a month's time, and they told me to bring someone."

Presenting the invitation obviously caused him anxiety. He lacked Joe's confidence, but that wasn't a bad thing. I was flattered and slightly flabbergasted.

"It's okay, you can think about it if you like."

I needed to respond. Not leave him hanging. I drew a breath and said I'd love to go.

"Great. I'll get the details to you when I have them."

"Okay."

I didn't plan on telling Graham and Marie about the invitation, but they sensed I was distracted. When I finally told them, they were happy for me and wanted to meet Robert. I assured them there was nothing in it—I was just going to his Christmas party as a friend, but their amused reaction suggested there was more to it. My racing heart suggested they might be right.

Despite telling myself that Robert had just invited me because he didn't know anyone else, underneath I began to hope it might be more than that. But was I truly ready for anything more than friendship? Had I dealt with all my issues? And what baggage was he carrying? I prayed about it and promised God that this time I would trust Him. I would not race into a new relationship without being sure it was what He wanted for me. But every time I thought about Robert, my pulse skittered.

The midweek meeting couldn't come quickly enough. When I arrived on time, I glanced around the room and my heart fell— he wasn't there. I chose a seat beside my friend from playgroup and began chatting with her and her husband, but my gaze flicked to the door every time someone walked in. When he followed another couple in, my flesh tingled as our gazes met and he gave a nod. Aware of his presence the whole evening, I struggled to focus on the study. When it ended, we found our way to each other and began to chat, but it wasn't like before. This time, something drew us together, and so, when he invited me to meet for coffee during the week, I accepted without hesitation. I wanted to get to know him. He seemed a good man, he loved the Lord, and a tangible bond was growing between us.

We met for coffee two days later and talked about so many things that coffee extended into lunch. As Robert walked me to my car a little later, he stopped, cleared his throat, and invited me to dinner. *A date.* I accepted. I'm not sure how I made it home, but I was totally entranced by him. Although twelve years older than me, it didn't seem to matter—we got on so well. I was floating on a soft, fluffy cloud.

Over the following weeks, we spent a lot of time together. He often dropped by the house, bearing chocolate eclairs and flowers. By the time his Christmas party came around, we were in love. Happy tears still spring to my eyes when I remember those days. God had brought us together, and we complemented each other so well. It didn't worry Robert that I had three young daughters, an ex-husband who could turn up at any moment, nor that I was bankrupt. We grew to love each other so much and knew that we could surmount any challenges that might come our way.

After several months of dating, Robert proposed. It was a whirlwind romance, but we both knew it was right, and I said yes right away. I'd prayed about this so much, and the girls loved him. His boys seemed to like me, although they were quiet and said little. There were seven years between his youngest son and Katie. We knew there'd be challenges ahead, but we agreed to face them together and with God.

Our friends and my family were pleased but voiced concern about how we'd manage with five children under the one roof. We told them we'd be fine. I felt truly thankful that I'd finally found someone who loved me as much as I loved him.

Our wedding day came, and it rained. It didn't matter. It was a low-key wedding, with the reception at my parents' home. Friends from my past came to celebrate with us—Sandy, my good friend from Sydney, Matt and Suzi from Dalby Cornerstone, and Sue, my wonderful friend from Bourke. Such special people God had placed in my life. I was so blessed.

Katie and Lily were my flower girls. They looked so cute in the little dresses I'd made for them. Sandy was my bridesmaid. As I walked down the aisle on my father's arm towards the wonderful man God had given me, I was blissfully happy and filled with anticipation for what lay ahead. Never could I have imagined when I drove away from the house in Bourke and left Joe forever, that in such a short time I'd be marrying the man of my dreams. But I'd learned that God only wants good things for His children, and if we're patient and trust Him, He truly does work all things out for good.

The hymn we chose for our wedding was one that reflected how we felt about God's provision and blessing in our lives:

Great is Thy faithfulness!
Great is Thy faithfulness!
Morning by morning new mercies I see;

All I have needed Thy hand hath provided—
Great is Thy faithfulness, Lord, unto me!

ROBERT NEVER DID FIND a job in his chosen field. After returning to teaching for a short time, I helped him with his business, and together we developed and ran a successful financial practice for over twenty years.

Although we've had our share of problems over our almost thirty years of marriage, we're still in love and have enjoyed so many wonderful experiences together. He's a good, hard-working, honest man. Our five children have all married and we now have many grandchildren who bring us great joy. I thank God every day for bringing Robert into my life.

Joe never bothered us. It still amazes me that I never met up with him again after that day he left to play tennis. For years after Robert and I married, I wondered if he'd turn up on the doorstep one day—it wouldn't have been hard to find us.

I kept in contact with his sisters, who told me he finally surfaced several months after the divorce went through. Over the following years, they kept me updated on his whereabouts, just in case. To his dying day, he remained a sad alcoholic, living mainly in shared accommodation. He occasionally went into rehab to dry out, but always returned to the bottle.

As the girls grew older, they seemed disinterested in knowing anything about him. However, when Elisha was sixteen, she wanted to meet him. I was concerned, especially as she was taking more of an interest in her indigenous heritage than her sisters. Not that I discouraged it, I just hadn't gone out of my way to encourage it, and I was hoping she wouldn't get caught up with the Aboriginal Rights movement. Going through a rebellious stage, she had some issues with Robert being her step-dad, even though he was the only dad she'd known, but I couldn't stop her from seeing Joe if she really wanted to.

We discussed it at length, and Robert and I finally agreed to go with her—not to see Joe, but to drive with her to his father's place where he was staying at that time, drop her off, and then pick her up again an hour later. She took a friend with her for support, which we were glad about. We weren't comfortable about her going on her own.

When we dropped her off at the corner of the street, we wished her well and said we'd be back in an hour. We also told her to call us if she wanted picking up before then. Robert and I found a café and waited nervously for the hour to pass. When we returned, she was already waiting for us. While she and her friend climbed into the car, I caught a glimpse of Joe standing on the front steps waving goodbye to her–the only time since that day in Bourke that I'd seen him. He wore a grey, straggly beard and looked generally unkempt. The good looks of his younger days were long gone.

It was the best thing that could have happened. When Elisha told Robert she was so glad that he was her dad and not Joe, tears sprung to my eyes. Their relationship improved from that day on. She'd seen for herself why I'd left him. He'd made an effort to be sober for her visit, but she knew he was itching for a drink. He told her that he hadn't had a proper job since the day I left, and that I was the best thing that had happened to him, and he knew he'd messed up.

He also told her that although he knew we'd gone to

Western Australia, he'd decided to let us be after the initial shock wore off. Maybe he had, maybe he hadn't, but what a relief that after all those years of torment, I was completely free of him.

Katie met up with him a few years later at a party the girls had been invited to by one of their cousins. She held few, if any, fond memories of her father. He was there, but although Elisha spoke to him for a short while, he didn't approach Katie —he just looked at her from a distance. I can only imagine what was going through his mind. His girls were all grown up, and he'd missed it all.

He died five years ago of a heart attack brought on by alcoholism. Despite having little to do with him and the way he treated them, the girls wanted to attend his funeral, but asked if Robert and I would go with them for support. We agreed, and I even provided photos to contribute to the audio-visual presentation his family compiled.

As I sat in the pew clinging to Robert's hand, I couldn't have been prouder of my girls. They'd been through so much in their childhood years, but God had protected them and made them into beautiful young women. I felt so sad for Joe. He'd missed out on so much, but it had been of his choosing. He'd caused his own demise by not allowing people to help him, nor allowing God to change his heart. So much potential, wasted.

I now understand that God only works in people's lives when they allow Him to. He doesn't force Himself onto anyone, but He longs for all to repent and turn to Him, and it breaks His heart when they shun Him and choose to live life without Him. He only wants the best for them, but so often people consider what they might have to give up to follow Him, and choose not to. They're deceived and don't know what they're missing out on. *'The thief comes only to steal and kill and destroy; I have come that they may have life, and have it to the full.'*

After all I went through with Joe, I praise God for the new life He's given me. So many wonderful blessings for which I'm truly grateful. I sometimes wonder what my life would have been like had I sought help after Greg ended our relationship instead of wallowing for years with a broken heart, or if I hadn't married Joe. Pivotal moments that changed the course of my life. Hindsight is a wonderful thing, but none of us can go back. I have so many 'should haves' and 'shouldn't haves', but the experiences I've been through have shaped my life, and I think they've all made me a better person.

God protected me through those years and taught me to trust Him, and then led me to a wonderful man to share my life with. I couldn't be happier or more grateful.

'But I trust in Your unfailing love; my heart rejoices in Your salvation. I will sing the Lord's praise, for He has been good to me.'

EPILOGUE

Julie's story is an interesting one, I'm sure you'll agree. All the more interesting, perhaps, because it's actually my own true story. Yes, the names are changed for privacy purposes, but the story is mine—I married my "Joe" after carrying a broken heart for years. I should have sought help to get over my breakup with "Greg", but I didn't.

If I could write a letter to my twenty-two-year-old self, I would have said something like this…

"Be secure in God's love and don't rush into marriage just because you might be lonely or doubt you'll ever find 'Mr. Right.' Trust God with all your heart because He only wants the best for you, and He has a wonderful plan for your life. Be patient, and trust Him."

However, I can't go back, and my years with "Joe", although tumultuous and challenging, drew me closer to God and strengthened my faith. I had to trust that He had a plan for my life, and that I had 'hope and a future'. Without this hope, I would have sunk into a deep depression.

I sincerely hope Julie's story touched your heart. My purpose in bringing you this story is to offer hope if you find yourself in a difficult situation, whatever it might be. I know what it's like to have a broken heart, to make poor decisions and then try to make them right. To live in fear, and to be committed to someone who continually hurts you, emotionally, physically, and financially.

I stayed with Joe, because although I knew I'd made a mistake when I married him, I believed in the sanctity of marriage. I couldn't leave him forever until I knew in my heart that I'd done everything possible to help him. Maybe that was foolish of me, and I should have stayed away the very first time I left. Had I done, I could have spared myself so much heartache. I didn't, but I praise God that I finally made the break with the help of some wonderful people, and was able to forge a new life for myself and my daughters.

If you're in a difficult situation, I want you to know that there's *always hope*. I was blessed to have so many people willing to help me. I can't promise the same for you, but be assured that God only wants the best for you, and if you need to escape a toxic relationship, please seek help. God doesn't expect you to suffer just because of a bad decision. If you live in fear of someone, seek help. Learn 'tough love'. Read good books, become a better, stronger person. Know that you're loved. I know that some women feel trapped and unable to do anything about their situation. Believe me, I know what that's like, but there's always a solution—you just have to look for it.

My dad told me that a leopard never changes his spots. In my ex-husband's case, he was right. It doesn't have to be that way, but I've learned that the only spots anyone has control over are their own. That doesn't mean you should lose hope for others, or stop praying. God will keep knocking on loved ones' hearts all the while someone is praying for them, but it's up to each individual to listen and respond. Sometimes, sadly, they don't respond when we want them to, but that doesn't mean they never will. I don't know if "Joe" ever truly gave his heart to God, but I have hope that even in his dying hours, he might have.

I believe that if anyone is truly open to God's amazing love, He can change their spots into whatever He wants. He can change a drunk into a preacher, and a prostitute into a missionary. He's in the business of changing lives. Of making good out of bad. Of providing hope when all hope seems lost.

My prayer is that you'll draw strength from Him, and claim Jeremiah chapter 29 verse 11 for yourself:

"For I know the plans I have for you," declares the Lord, "plans to prosper you and not to harm you, plans to give you hope and a future."

'May the Lord bless you and keep you; the Lord make His face shine on you and be gracious to you; the Lord turn His face toward you and give you peace.' Amen.

Much love,

Juliette

Join Juliette's List and never miss a new release or a special sale on her books.

http://www.julietteduncan.com/linkspage/282748

This may have been the first book of mine that you've read. I started writing full-time in 2015 after my husband and I sold our business. I mainly write contemporary Christian romances, but not the light, fluffy type. I believe that God has called me to write stories that touch the heart and draw readers closer to God, not just entertain. Whilst they might not be "suspense" in the true sense of the word, my stories are real, and if you've enjoyed my own story, I think you'll enjoy my made up ones!

Read on for a sneak peek of "**The Shadows Series**". This series is very loosely based on my own story. Lizzy, the main protagonist, is a school teacher whose heart has been broken by her student minister beau. Daniel is a rogue Irishman with a drinking problem he keeps hidden from her. The series is set in England, Ireland and Scotland, and although there are similarities to my own story, it's a work of fiction that tells of God's amazing grace. Here's your sneak peek. Read it now, and then I'd love it if you went on and bought the boxset. http://www.julietteduncan.com/linkspage/186278 Enjoy!

North East England 1981

Marrying Daniel O'Connor was a risk, no two ways about it. Lizzy still didn't know why she'd agreed to marry him, but tomorrow at midday, come what may, she would be saying "I do".

Although impetuous, she was also loyal, and while her actions were highly irregular, she *would* see it through, and she *would* be a good wife to Daniel, regardless of what anyone thought. And she'd prove her father wrong.

She would also ask God to bless their marriage, even though Daniel didn't yet share her beliefs.

THE PAST WEEK had been busy, keeping her mind off tomorrow, and now she had to collect Sal, her best and most loyalist of friends, from the station. Lizzy glanced at her watch and tapped her fingers on the steering wheel as the traffic stalled in front of her.

"Come on, you lot! I don't want to be late. Move!" She thumped the wheel, and then sped around the car in front that had completely stopped and was going nowhere.

The train pulled into the station just as she entered the car park. She zipped into a spot someone had just vacated, jumped out of the car, slammed the door, and sprinted to the entrance, taking the stairs two at a time. People of all sizes and shapes were already piling out of the train onto the platform, but Sal's carrot red hair stood out amongst the crowd, making her easy to spot.

"Sal!" Lizzy waved and called out, not worried in the slightest what the people around her would think. Running down the stairs against the general flow of traffic, she bumped into anyone who wasn't fast enough to get out of her way, and almost knocked Sal off her feet when, finally reaching her, she threw her arms around her best friend with uncontrolled abandon.

"I'm so glad you could make it, Sal. It's great to see you!" Lizzy whirled her around and hugged her again.

"Wow Liz! It's great to see you too, but it's only been three months!" Sal drew her eyebrows together and tilted her head slightly, curiosity loitering in her smile as she searched Lizzy's face. "Are you okay?"

Lizzy pulled back, annoyed at Sal's perception. "Of course I'm okay. What makes you think I'm not?"

"Oh, you just seem a little on edge."

Lizzy's eyes narrowed and her lips flattened into a thin line as she picked up Sal's dark brown carry all.

"I'm fine."

"Okay then." Sal glanced at Lizzy from the corner of her eye before tucking her arm through the crook of Lizzy's elbow as they walked back along the platform. "I still can't believe you moved all the way up here. Couldn't you have gone somewhere just a little closer?"

"You know why I did." Lizzy breathed in deeply. "Oh, but Sal, I do miss home." Lizzy fought back the sudden tears that pricked her eyes, and then turned her head to Sal, a forced smile planted on her face. "But enough of that. Tell me everything that's been happening."

All the way to the car, the girls chatted like two long lost friends, and Lizzy's mind was taken off the events of the morrow yet again.

THE TRAFFIC HADN'T LESSENED, and as she pulled out of the car park, Lizzy turned on the wipers. *A wet day. Great. That's all I need.*

She slammed on the brakes as a car pulled out in front of her, and blasted the horn while she shouted at the driver, a futile exercise, but it made her feel better. Her nerves were a little on edge.

"You haven't told your parents yet, have you?"

Lizzy bristled and held the steering wheel a little tighter. *Why did Sal have to bring my parents up?* She shook her head without looking at Sal.

"Don't you think you should?"

Lizzy clenched her jaw. *Why can't she let things be? Maybe asking her to come was a mistake.* But Sal was her best friend.

She put her foot down to beat the lights that had just changed to amber. "No. And I don't feel bad about it. They'd never agree to me marrying him, so I'm just going to do it. I know they'll be angry when they find out, but it'll be too late to do anything about it then. They shouldn't have been so horrible to him."

"Are you sure you know what you're doing, Liz? Have you prayed about it?"

Sal's eyes bored into her. Lizzy wasn't game to look. *Maybe I should tell her how I'm really feeling.* But if she knew the truth, Lizzy was sure that Sal would try her best to stop her from marrying Daniel, and it wasn't worth the risk. Having set her path, Lizzy was determined to stick to it. She'd actually contemplated calling it off a few times over the past couple of weeks, but the prospect of being alone again made her banish those thoughts immediately. It had to be better to be with someone than to be lonely.

Lizzy took a deep breath and calmed herself. "Yes, I've prayed about it. And yes, I do love him. I know what I'm doing, Sal, even if you think I don't." She slowed down to take the next corner. "He's a bit of a lad, so different to Mathew, but I love him. He makes me laugh and smile. I feel happy when I'm with him." She turned her head and glanced at Sal. "I know what you're thinking, and you might be right. I probably am marrying him on the rebound, but you know what? I don't care. I can't handle being on my own any longer." She wiped the tears from her eyes and hoped Sal hadn't seen them.

Sal looked at her intently. "I hope you'll be happy, Liz. I really do."

THEY SAT QUIETLY the rest of the way to Lizzy's apartment on the outskirts of town. The street lights had come on early, and the drizzle had increased to light rain. The windscreen wipers were doing their thing, and their squeak reminded Lizzy she needed to get new blades.

"This is it. Home sweet home." Lizzy pointed to the block of apartments on the left as she reversed into a small gap on the narrow street lined with cars. Four storeys high, and spanning half a block, the complex's only redeeming feature was the garden that ran between the brown brick walls and the footpath. "It's better on the inside," she said as she saw the look on Sal's face.

"I would hope so!" Sal raised her eyebrows. "A bit of a come down, Liz. "Are you going to live here once you're married?"

"For a while. It really is much better on the inside." Lizzy opened the car door and climbed out. She zipped her jacket and covered her head with its hood before grabbing Sal's bags out of the boot and directing her up the flight of stairs. Opening the door to the apartment, she held her breath as she waited for Sal's reaction.

"Wow, Liz! You weren't wrong! This really is nice!" Sal entered the living room and fell onto the new sofa Lizzy had picked up recently at a sale. "You always did have an eye for nice things."

"Thanks Sal." Lizzy's face expanded into a broad grin. "I'll just put these in your room and then make us a drink."

Lizzy placed Sal's bags in the spare room, and then busied herself making a cup of tea. She glanced at the clock. Daniel would be here any minute.

"LIZ! I know you told me he was good looking, but you didn't tell me how much!"

"Shh! He'll hear you!"

"Okay, I'll just sit here and drool."

"He is pretty cute, I have to agree." Lizzy laughed and glanced over to where Daniel was standing at the bar, and her heart warmed. Maybe she did love him after all.

"Here you go, my lovelies! Two shandies with flair!" Daniel placed the glasses on the table and winked at Sal.

"Daniel! You shouldn't do that! What will she think!" Lizzy said with a laugh in her voice.

"Oh, go on," he said in his best Irish accent. "I was just having a bit o' fun!"

"It's okay, Liz." Sal patted Lizzy's leg and then looked up, a warm smile on her face. "Thank you, kind sir."

"My pleasure." He bowed, and then took his seat beside Lizzy. He placed his arm around her shoulders, and pulled her close. She didn't resist, instead, she snuggled closer.

"Good of you to come up for the wedding, Sal," Daniel said. "Lizzy's told me a lot about you."

"Has she just?" Sal glanced at Lizzy with a glint of mischief in her eye. "And what exactly has she been saying?"

"Oh, only good things," Daniel replied.

"I'm pleased to hear that!" Sal said.

"And what has she told you about me?" Daniel raised his eyebrows.

Sal hesitated and stole a glance at Lizzy before replying. "Only good things!"

Both girls burst out in laughter at Sal's attempt to copy his accent. Lizzy sat up and smiled at Daniel. As their eyes met, a tingle of excitement ran through her body. Cheeky he might be, but he was also lovable. And he was going to be her husband.

"Come on you two! You'll have enough time for that tomorrow!" Sal said.

Lizzy turned her head and grinned at Sal. "Yes, you're right. Let's order, shall we?"

As Lizzy laughed and reminisced with Sal over dinner, her heart lightened and her anxiety over her forthcoming wedding lessened. For a while at least.

When she climbed into bed a few hours later, however, her active mind kept her awake. Did she really know what she was doing?

I hope you enjoyed your sneak peek you can purchase "The Shadows Series" or read for FREE on Kindle Unlimited. http://www.julietteduncan.com/linkspage/186278 Check out my other books on the next page.

OTHER BOOKS BY JULIETTE DUNCAN

Find all of Juliette Duncan's books on her website: www. julietteduncan.com/library

Water's Edge Series

When I Met You

A barmaid searching for purpose, a youth pastor searching for love

Because of You

When dreams are shattered, can hope be re-found?

A Sunburned Land Series

A mature-age romance series

Slow Road to Love

A divorced reporter on a remote assignment. An alluring cattleman who captures her heart…

Slow Path to Peace

With their lives stripped bare, can Serena and David find peace?

Slow Ride Home

He's a cowboy who lives his life with abandon. She's spirited and fiercely independent…

Slow Dance at Dusk

A death, a wedding, and a change of plans…

Slow Trek to Triumph

A road trip, a new romance, and a new start…

The Shadows Series

A jilted teacher, a charming Irishman, & the chance to escape their pasts & start again.

Lingering Shadows

Facing the Shadows

Beyond the Shadows

Secrets and Sacrifice

A Highland Christmas

True Love Series

Tender Love

Tested Love

Tormented Love

Triumphant Love

Precious Love Series

Forever Cherished

Forever Faithful

Forever His

A Time For Everything Series

A mature-age Christian Romance series

A Time to Treasure

She lost her husband and misses him dearly. He lost his wife but is ready to move on. Will a chance meeting in a foreign city change their lives forever?

A Time to Care

They've tied the knot, but will their love last the distance?

A Time to Abide

When grief hovers like a cloud, will the sun ever shine again for Wendy?

A Time to Rejoice

He's never forgiven himself for the accident that killed his mother. Can he find forgiveness and true love?

Transformed by Love Christian Romance Series

Because We Loved

Because We Forgave

Because We Dreamed

Because We Believed

Because We Cared

Billionaires with Heart Series

Her Kind-Hearted Billionaire

A reluctant billionaire, a grieving young woman, and the trip *that changes their lives forever...*

Her Generous Billionaire

A grieving billionaire, a devoted solo mother, and a woman determined to sabotage their relationship...

Her Disgraced Billionaire

A billionaire in jail, a nurse who cares, and the challenge that changes their lives forever...

Her Compassionate Billionaire

A widowed billionaire with three young children. A replacement nanny who helps change his life…

The Potter's House Books...

Stories of hope, redemption, and second chances. *The Homecoming*

Can she surrender a life of fame and fortune to find true love?

Blessings of Love

She's going on mission to help others. He's going to win her heart.

The Hope We Share

Can the Master Potter work in Rachel and Andrew's hearts and give them a second chance at love?

The Love Abounds

Can the Master Potter work in Megan's heart and save her marriage?

Love's Healing Touch

A doctor in need of healing. A nurse in need of love.

Melody of Love

She's fleeing an abusive relationship, he's grieving his wife's death…

Whispers of Hope

He's struggling to accept his new normal. She's losing her patience…

Heroes Of Eastbrooke Christian Suspense Series

Safe in His Arms

SOME SAY HE'S HIDING. HE SAYS HE'S SURVIVING

Under His Watch

HE'LL STOP AT NOTHING TO PROTECT THOSE HE LOVES. NOTHING.

Within His Sight

SHE'LL STOP AT NOTHING TO GET A STORY. HE'LL SCALE

THE HIGHEST MOUNTAIN TO RESCUE HER.

Freed by His Love

HE'S DRIVEN AND DETERMINED. SHE'S BROKEN AND SCARED.

Stand Alone Christian Romantic Suspense

Leave Before He Kills You

When his face grew angry, I knew he could murder…

The Madeleine Richards Series

Although the 3 book series is intended mainly for pre-teen/Middle Grade girls, it's been read and enjoyed by people of all ages. Here's what one reader had to say about it: *"Juliette has a fabulous way of bringing her characters to life. Maddy is at typical teenager with authentic views and actions that truly make it feel like you are feeling her pain and angst. You want to enter into her situation and make everything better. Mom and soon to be dad respond to her with love and gentle persuasion while maintaining their faith and trust in Jesus, whom they know, will give them wisdom as they continue on their lives journey. Appropriate for teenage readers but any age can enjoy." Reader*

ABOUT THE AUTHOR

Juliette Duncan is a USA Today bestselling author of Christian romance stories that 'touch the heart and soul'. She lives in Brisbane, Australia and writes Christian fiction that encourages a deeper faith in a world that seems to have lost its way. Most of her stories include an element of romance, because who doesn't love a good love story? But the main love story in each of her books is always God's amazing, unconditional love for His wayward children.

Juliette and her husband enjoy spending time with their five adult children, eight grandchildren, and their elderly, long-haired dachshund, Chipolata (Chip for short). When not writing, Juliette and her husband love exploring the wonderful world they live in.

Connect with Juliette:

Email: juliette@julietteduncan.com

Website: www.julietteduncan.com

Facebook: www.facebook.com/JulietteDuncanAuthor

Printed in Great Britain
by Amazon